tuned in

EPISODE #4

music
mania

by Julia DeVillers

introduction

Hi! It's me, Maddy! And OK, I'm here surrounded by lots of girls! WAY lots of girls! I mean, BAJILLIONS of girls! Girls who are laughing and screaming and singing and dancing ...!

Why?!!

Because I'm here at a concert!

And not just any concert! Noooo, this is SO not just any ordinary concert. It's a HUMONGOUS music festival with lots of famous singers and groups. It's called Toopalooza. As in TOOpalooza. As in Limited TOO.

And I'm here! Right in the middle of the crowd!

Is it because I'm some special famous and glamorous person or something?

Nope! I'm just me, regular Maddy Elizabeth Sparks!

I'm here with the TOO Crew!

Kacey is singing along with the music group on stage!

Isabel is dancing along with the music group on stage!

Claire is freaking out because her #1 Celebrity Crush was right on that stage!!!!

So how cool is this?!!!

WAYYYYYY Cool!

AHHHHHHHHHHHHH! That's me screaming! With everyone else! We're all like AHHHHHHHHHH!

I can't believe it's real. I mean, a couple days ago I was at my new school stressing out! Bumming out! Feeling left out!

But now ...

I'M AT TOOPALOOZA!!!!!!!!!

THIS ROCKS!!!!!!!!

How did this all happen?

OK, let me tell you the deal!!!!

chapter 1

This Journal Belongs to:

Maddy Elizabeth Sparks

PRIVATE!   KEEP
                                            OUT!!!

No Little Brothers Allowed!

OK! I have a MAJOR decision to make!!!

Should I try out for cheerleading? Yes or No?

So here's the deal. I already tried out for cheerleading once before. That was football cheerleading. Did all of my friends from school make it? Yup, sure did. Did I make it? Nope. That's a big N-O.

But now, I have another chance. I can try out for basketball cheerleading.

Soooooo ... should I try out?!?!?!

Reason I DON'T want to try out:

I don't want to be embarrassed AGAIN. (I can hear everyone now. "Poor Maddy didn't make the team AGAIN! Why did she even bother!!")

Reason I WANT to try out:

My friends are trying out! And I don't want to be left out of everything again!!!!

But also, really ...

I want to be a cheerleader! I like cheerleading! I like the jumping and the flipping and the yelling and the chanting and the dancing and when the music's cranked up and we're all clapping and stamping at just the right moment together and we're all going to pump up the crowd and it's awesome!

I just really like to cheerlead!

Too bad I STINK at it. And I do. I must be bad, bad, bad. Totally hopeless. Or else I would have made the team the first time ... right?

So anyway. I probably shouldn't try out, right? Probably not. Maybe. OK. Yeah.

The answer is NO. I will not try out for cheerleading.

OK. That's my decision. I think.

I was sitting in my Language Arts class. We're studying "Speeches." For homework, our assignment was to do our own speech about yourself called, *This Is Really Me.*

And now we have *"share with the class."* Ugh.

I hate *"share with the class."* I hate standing up there and everyone's looking at you. Or else they're not looking at you, which means you're boring them. That's bad, too.

Anyway, either one stinks. Shana was up there finishing her speech. It was good. She talked about how she wanted to be a marine biologist. And she was showing a video of her swimming with dolphins on vacation. It was cool. I hope I didn't get called on next. Mine wasn't so good compared to hers. Mine was like "I have a brother and a guinea pig" blah blah boring boring.

It would put everyone to sleep. For sure.

There were only a couple minutes left in class. Maybe I wouldn't have to do mine today. I could rewrite it tonight and make it better! Yeah! That's what I'll do!

Clap, clap, clap for Shana. Shana sat down.

My teacher, Miss Flocksum, started to talk.

"OK, our next speech on *This Is Really Me* will be from ..."

Don't call on me don't call on me don't call on me don't call on ...

"Maddy Sparks."

Me!

DARN!! RATS!!! AUGH! It's me. She called on me. OK.

OK!

OK! My turn! I'm up! I grabbed my papers! I jumped up! OK!
OK! I started walking up to the front of the class. Up the aisle!
OK, try not to be nervous. OK, OK. Keep going, step over
Quinn's backpack, keep going! But oh no ... wait a minute ...

My sneaker was caught in her backpack strap! I went like
"WHOA!!!!"

And then I was tripping up the aisle! I was falling! My speech
papers were flying up in the air! ACK! There were papers flying
everywhere! I stepped on a slippery piece of paper and oh no!

I was sliding across the front of the room! Hang on, Maddy!
Steady yourself! I grabbed wildly at Miss Flocksum's desk!

But WHAM! I knocked her mug full of pencils into the air.

Freshly sharpened pencils were flying everywhere!

"Duck, students, duck!" Miss Flocksum yelled!

Everyone was screaming ACK! They were covering their heads from flying pencils! They were jumping under desks for cover!

And then BAM! I landed, finally. On the floor. I looked out at the classroom. It was all of a sudden quiet. Everyone was peeking out from under their arms. And their desks.

And then they all started laughing.

At me. Of course!

OK, Maddy. Recover. You've embarrassed yourself before. Say something funny. Do something to recover. Um! Um! UM!!!!

BBBBRRRRRRRrrrrrrrrrrrrrrrrrannnnnng!

Dismissal bell! Everyone ran out of class. Laughing. Really loud. I heard someone go, "How embarrassing was THAT?!!"

AUGH! I DIDN'T GET TO RECOVER!!!!

"Maddy," Mrs. Flocksum said to me, from the floor where she was picking up pencils. "We'll have to do your speech next class."

✳ ✳✳✳✳✳ ✳

I walked to the bus really fast. Looking down. Hiding my face so nobody would laugh when they saw me. I'd just spent my last two classes at the nurse's office. Hiding out on a cot with a sheet over my head.

"You don't have a temperature," the nurse told me when I told her I was, uh, too sick to go to class. "But your face IS unnaturally red. Maybe you should lie down for a bit."

I heard someone in the hall go, "And then she tripped! And stuff was flying everywhere! And ... "

AUGH!

This was a baaaaaaaaad day. A reallllllllly baaaaaaaad day. I practically ran to the bus. Not that the bus was going to be any better. The afternoon bus ride has been the WORST! Why? I am a total BUS LOSER! Meaning: I sit alone!

In the morning I don't. I sit with Danielle. Brittany and Haley sit in front of me, just like last year. But this year, all my friends from my bus were staying after school every day for cheerleading stuff. And I have nobody to sit with on the way home!!!

NOBODY!

The first day, the bus ride was pretty bad. I got on the bus. I walked real slow. Pretending to be looking for somebody. Like, oh friends who are saving me a seat, where are you! Because I have many friends to sit with, and I just need to spot them!

I was soooo hoping somebody would call out, "Hey Maddy! Sit with me!" But nobody did. WAH!

So I plopped down in a seat ... ALL BY MYSELF!! I felt like everybody was thinking, That girl is a bus loser!!!

But today, for once, that wasn't such a bad thing. I could sit by myself. And hide from my humiliation!!!!

I got on the bus.

"Maddy! I saved you a seat!" someone yelled. It was Danielle! And in front of her was Brittany and Haley! At least none of them were in my Language Arts class.

"Hey! You're taking the bus!" I said. I slid in next to Danielle.

"Cheerleading practice got canceled at the last minute," Danielle said. "So here we are!"

Brittany's head popped over the seat. "So, you guys! Did you hear the sign up sheet for basketball cheer tryouts is going up TOMORROW?! I'm sooo nervous!"

Brittany's mom is the cheerleading coach. Brittany is co-captain of the football cheerleading team. Brittany has been taking cheerleading since she was six. So I'm thinking she doesn't have to be too nervous.

"Are you going to try out?" Danielle asked me.

But before I could say anything, Brittany goes, "Well, Maddy didn't make it last time. So she probably doesn't want to go through that humiliation again."

OK, yes, well. It's true. But she didn't have to put it like that!

"Well," I said. "Jordan Cooper didn't make it either and she told me today she was going to try out again."

And then Brittany waved her hand and made a noise like Phhht! Jordan Cooper! Brittany so doesn't like Jordan Cooper. But I do. I sit with Jordan at lunch now.

"Maddy's probably too busy for cheerleading, anyway," Brittany said. "With the music fest coming up and everything."

Ooooohkay. Brittany was still not too happy about the *TOO's U-Pick Challenge* Contest. The stuff we did to help get ready for the Toopalooza music fest. I was on the winning team. Brittany was on the losing team.

Brittany doesn't like to be on the losing team. Ever. I haven't seen Brittany too much since the contest. She's been cheerleading. I've been staying out of her way. I didn't want to rub it in about winning. Or going to Toopalooza!

(I can't believe Toopalooza is coming and I'm going to be there!!! It just doesn't seem real!)

"Did your mom say how many spots there were going to be?" Danielle asked Brittany.

"Same as football cheerleading. So that means, if someone new makes it, then somebody on the team now would be goners." Brittany made a slicing motion across her neck. Like CUT!

"Ohmigosh! That would be way bad!" Haley said.

"Well," said Danielle. "It would be a bummer. But it also would give some other girls a chance to cheerlead who didn't get to before."

Brittany hung over the seat, right in Danielle's face.

"Well, I did hear my mom say maybe it wouldn't be so bad to have some new girls come on board. Since there are a couple girls who aren't doing so great ..."

Danielle shrunk down in her seat. I knew what she was thinking. Maybe that meant her! She'd shown me her bruises from falling off the pyramid.

"So!" Brittany continued. "I'm thinking of doing a new routine for my tryout. My private cheer tutor showed it to me. It has this double back handspring in it! How hype is that? I'm the only girl on the team who can do a double back handspring."

I think I have another reason I might NOT want to try out for basketball cheerleading: If I make the team, I would have to spend a lot more time with Brittany, co-captain of the cheerleaders!

And sometimes, that is so NOT a good thing!

"Besides," Brittany was saying cheerfully. "Maddy's suffered enough humiliation lately, right Maddy? Did you guys hear what happened in her Lang Arts class? Alyssa told me that Katie told her that ..."

Oh nooooooooooo!

Brittany was telling Haley and Danielle about it. Tripping! Falling! Sharp pointy pencils flying like missiles! Even Danielle was cracking up.

"Sorry, Maddy," she said. "But it is pretty funny."

The bus pulled on to my street.

"OK, well, yeah," I mumbled, all feeling stupid. "There's my stop."

"Byeeeee, Maddy!" Brittany, Haley and Danielle waved at me.

I rushed down the aisle. I just wanted OUT of there! I needed to get this day OVER!

I ran down the step but then oh no! I tripped on the top step! I fell! Right on the girl in front of me!

Whoops!

Red-face Rating: ★★☆☆ out of ★★★★☆ stars.
I wanted a trip home ON the bus. Not to trip OFF the bus.

"Sorry! Sorry!" I said to the girl. She gave me a look like, OW!

I heard Brittany and Haley cracking up. Oh ha. Ha ha.

"Maddy!" I heard Brittany say. "Have a nice TRIP to the music fest. Get it, have a nice TRIP?!!! See you next FALL?!! Ha ha ha ..."

I started walking to my house. That's it. I am never going back to school. And just forget about cheerleading. Today was a sign. A sign of what a SuperKlutz I am. And SuperKlutzes should not try out for cheerleading. Too embarrassing. I mean, who needs rejection, right? If I don't go, I don't have to worry about it.

I might HAVE to go back to school. But I don't HAVE to try out for cheerleading. So. Nope. I'm not.

chapter 2

I stopped at my mailbox and pulled out the mail. I pulled out a bunch of junk mail and hey ... a catalog ....

Oh! My! GOSH!

There was my face. And Kacey's and Isabel's and Claire's.

THE LIMITED TOO CATAZINE WAS HERE! THE ONE WHERE I WAS ON THE COVER!!!!! WITH THE TOO CREW!!!!

How cool is THAT!

Way Way Wayest of Cool.

I was totally staring at it! I still can't believe I was a catazine model. But here was proof ... in my mailbox!!!

I suddenly was starting to feel better. I ran into the house. "MOM!" I yelled. "I'm home and I have something cool to show you!"

"Be down in a second, Maddy!" my mom called back. "Check the answering machine."

Our answering machine was blinking 2 new messages. I hit the PLAY button for the first message.

"Maddddddddy! Maddy Mad Mads!" I heard a voice shriek. It was Taylor! My BFF! "Guess what I got in the mail! The catazine! You look so awesome! I'm so psyched for you!!"

Yay! How cool is that that girls all over the country were opening their mailboxes and going, yay! My catazine is here. And there I, Maddy Elizabeth Sparks, am in it!

Beep!

"Hi, this is Jordan Cooper. I just got the new catazine in the mail. That is so cooooool! Anyway, I want to know if you want to practice some cheers with me for tryouts. Call me. Bye."

Oh yeah. Cheerleading.

I had to make up my mind about cheerleading. Should I try out? Or should I bail out?

I looked at the catazine in my hand. I remembered how I almost didn't even go to Limited Too that day. I got way nervous. I thought I'd totally screw it up. I almost just said, Forget about it! Not worth the trouble! Too many things could go wrong. I almost didn't go ...

... I was so glad I did.

I almost missed out on being part of the TOO Crew.

If I don't try out for cheerleading ... I guess I'll never know. I'll never know what I missed.

OK. Tomorrow, I'll do it. I'll sign up. To try out for cheerleading.

"How was your day, sweetie?" my mom asked, walking in.

"Uh, well, guess what, mom? The catazine is here!" I ran over to show her.

"Wonderful, sweetie," my mom said. "We'll have to get a frame."

I headed upstairs to my room. I flopped out on my bed with the catazine. I checked out the cover. Kacey, Isabel, Claire and I were kind of in a jumble on the floor. We were laughing. It was sooooo cool.

I flipped through a couple pages. Cool sweater. Flip flip. Cute pjs. Flip flip. Oh ...

Ugh. There was a picture that looked good ... that seemed good ... if I didn't know better. Because the models were Piper and Sierra! Blugh. Piper and Sierra were these two girls that were ...

RUDE! And NASTY! SNOBBY! And seriously not nice. Hmm, maybe I should draw mustaches on their pictures.

Just kidding.

Kinda.

I flipped to another page. Hey! There's Alexa! Alexa was another catazine model that day. Turns out she's a singer, too. A singer in my fave new band, INSPIRE. INSPIRE was the winner of *TOO's U-Pick Challenge* Contest, and will perform at Toopalooza!!!

Toopalooza!

Toopalooza is this huge music fest. With some of my favorite singers! And bands! And I get to go help out at it as part of the TOO Crew. Yes, me. Maddy Elizabeth Sparks!

AND I WOULD BE GOING THERE IN TWO DAYS!!!

I totally can't wait.Ican'twaitIcan'twaitIcan'twaitIcan'twait!

JIGGLE! JIGGLE! PUSH!

I heard a noise. It was my doorknob jiggling. My brother, Zack! Trying to get in my room! Oh nooooooo ....

"Go away, Zack!" I yelled. "My day was just getting better. Don't spoil it."

JIGGLE! JIGGLE! PUSH!

"Zack!" I yelled. "Can't you at least knock?!" Yeesh.

"No time for knocking," Zack yelled. "I've got scoop. Open up!"

Hm. When you have a little brother like Zack you just don't open the door. Because it could be a trick.

"Are you going to spray me with a squirt gun?" I asked.

"No!" he answered back.

"Do you have crazy string you're going to spray all over my head?"

"NO!"

"Slimy goo to throw at me? Slimy worms?"

"Oh, OK, hang on. I'll put the slimy goo in my room." I heard Zack's footsteps go away and then come back.

"OK, I'm clear! Open up!" Zack yelled.

I opened the door a crack and peeked out. Zack was holding up a newspaper.

He pushed past me into my room.

"Check this out, dude," Zack said. "I found this on the table. Dad left it out. And it was opened to this page." He pointed.

"New dog shelter opening next month!" the newspaper headline said. "Shelter will care for dogs until they're placed for adoption."

A dog shelter! Do you think ...? Does this mean ...?

Could it be true? Is dad thinking about getting a dog?!!!

Do I have a dog? No! Do I want a dog? Yes! Yes with extra YES!

Dad always said, No way, no how, no dog.

But then I dogsat for my neighbor's dog. Cute little foofy Scrumptious. And dad saw I could take care of a dog. And when I asked him if we could get one, what did I think he would say?

a) Sorry, no!
b) No way!
c) A big fat NO!

But instead he said ... I'll think about it.

Dad really and truly said, "I'll think about it!"

So I'm letting him think. Because I think I'll think about it means ... maybe soon ... it will be ... YES!

"I hope that means what I think it means!" I said.

"Me, too," said Zack. "I hope it means Jaws, He-Dog of the Universe is coming soon!"

What?

"Who's Jaws, He-Dog of the Universe?" I asked him.

"Duh," Zack said. "Our dog that we're going to get."

Maddy's favorite names for her dog (when she gets one!):

☆ Sunny
☆ Princess
☆ Cocoa
☆ Ginger

"We are NOT naming our dog Jaws, He-Dog of the Universe," I said. "That is so not even on the list."

"OK, OK, how 'bout Terror, Attack Dog Extreme."

"Out, Zack," I said. I closed the door on him. But his voice still kept coming.

"Beast, the King of the Animal World? Or Claw, the Mighty Dog of Doom?"

Augh! Just what I need! My cute snuggly dog I'm going to get someday named ... Claw?

So NOT.

"OK! Got it. Savage, Dog of Total Destruction!"

AUGH! I needed to block out his noise. I would crank up some tunes. I turned on my CD player and turned up the volume.

I would get in the mood for ... Toopalooza!!!! I put in my new INSPIRE CD and clicked my favorite song.

Happiness comes, And happiness goes.
But today is the day, My happiness grows.

Whenever I felt bummed out, that song cheered me up. So OK! I wasn't going to think about cheerleading tryouts. I wasn't going to think about Brittany. I wasn't going to think about tripping, falling, flying pencils and making the biggest idiot of myself in school today.

I was going to think about ... going to Toopalooza!

Times I have gone to a concert before:

- 0 (never in my life!!!)

My first concert. This was so major! I love music. I totally love music. Radio! CDs! Off my computer! I love slow songs! Fast songs! Medium songs!

I have pins of my favorite music groups all over my backpack. I have posters of my fave singers on my locker.

But I have never ... ever ... been to a concert before!

AHHHHHH!!!!!!!!!!!!

How excited am I?

0%————————————— 100% !!! 😊

Off the charts excited!

I can't believe I'm going to be in the same place as ...

★ Aaron Carter
★ Ashlee Simpson
★ Mandy Moore
★ Jessica Simpson
★ Play
★ Nick Cannon
★ Jhene
★ Nikki Cleary
★ INSPIRE

They'll be singing. They'll be dancing.

And I'm going to be like ...
AHHHHHHHHHHHHHHHHHHHH!!!

WOO HOO!!!

YEAH!!!!

I went over to my guinea pig's cage. I picked up Sugar.

"Squee? Squee?" she asked.

"I just have to get through tomorrow without dying of embarrassment," I told her. "Then in two days I will be OUTTA here. I will be at Toopalooza!" I told her. I danced around the room, with Sugar in my arms.

Things are looking up! Oh yeah!
Things are looking up!

chapter 3

This Journal Belongs to:

Maddy Elizabeth Sparks

So this is totally crazy! I'm on my way to Toopalooza! Mom and me took a plane to California. Because that's where Toopalooza is going to be!!!! It's at an amusement park called LEGOLAND®.

I remembered the last time I was in a plane going to California. The TOO Crew went to Hollywood to help with a contest. I sat next to Kacey! And near Isabel and Claire!

But this time, it was just me and mom on the plane. Kacey, Isabel, and Claire already flew out this afternoon. Mom and I had to come late tonight because of when Mrs. Hubert could get to our house to watch Zack.

I'd packed yesterday. I was in a better mood last night. Not only was I going to Toopalooza, but I didn't have to give my speech yesterday! Mrs. Flocksum was absent!

Of course, I still had to deal with everyone going, "Maybe Mrs. Flocksum had to stay home sick today 'cuz she got lead poisoning from pencils!" "Maybe Mrs. Flocksum had to go to the hospital 'cuz she got poked with a pencil point."

Oh, ha ha.

So that was not so fun. And also how at lunch when I sat down, Derek Hogan was telling everyone the story. And how Ryan Moore was sitting right there.

RYAN MOORE! #1 on my ULTIMATE CRUSH LIST!

Who probably thinks I'm the biggest dork now. I couldn't

even look at him the whole lunch period.

But OK! I am so not thinking about that anymore.

Because now ... I'm a batrillion miles away. In California! The plane ride is over! And now I'm in a taxi to the hotel!! It's dark out already. It's nighttime. Almost time to go to bed already. But when I wake up it will be ...

Toopalooza! And we're here!!!!!

I headed up to the hotel room with mom. Mom wheeled our suitcase. I carried my navy backpack. I couldn't wait to see Kacey, Isabel, and Claire. I hadn't seen them since the day of the *TOO's U-Pick Challenge* Contest. We'd all been busy with school starting and all.

The three of them all got here together. Took the plane together. Had dinner together. I felt ... a little nervous to see them. Which was weird, right? I mean, they're totally my friends and all. But ... they all came here together. What if they had the best time on the plane? And the hotel? What if they were like, "We're having so much fun together ... we didn't even notice Maddy wasn't here! Who needs Maddy? Maddy who?"

Wait a minute. That might happen with some of my friends at school. But you know what? That doesn't happen with the TOO Crew. They're always glad to see me!!!

But, still. What if I missed something? Something really fun?

I buzzed on the hotel buzzer.

BZZZZT!!!

I waited. And then ... the door opened ... and it was KACEY! And then ISABEL! And CLAIRE!!!

They were all hugging me! Screaming! AHHHHHHHHH!

"We're soooo glad you're here!" Kacey screamed.

"We missed you on the plane!" Claire said. "We missed you at dinner!"

"We just plain missed you!" Kacey screamed, even louder.

Yay!

"Get in here girl," Isabel said. "Welcome to the Too-Crew-Palooza!!"

We all were laughing!

YEAH! TOO-CREW-PALOOZA!

"Hi, Mrs. Sparks," everybody said to my mom as she walked in.

"Mrs. Sparks, your room is attached to ours over there," Isabel pointed to one of the three doors. "And Lauren's room is attached there. And my grandmother's room is attached there. She went to bed early. Bruno's somewhere down the hall."

Bruno works for Claire's father. He goes everywhere with her. He's really quiet. Even though he's a big guy, sometimes I forget he's even there!

There was a knock from one of the doors. And Lauren came in, holding a bag.

"Maddy!" she said, and gave me a hug. "I'm so glad you're here. It didn't seem complete without you today."

Aw!

"And tomorrow's coming fast, girls," Lauren said. "So I know you're excited to see Maddy. But why don't you head to bed soon and get some sleep. Tomorrow's going to be a big day."

The BIGGEST!

Lauren started to go back to her room. She was walking through the adjoining door. Then she turned around.

"But before you go to bed," she added. "If anyone has the munchies, the mini fridge is at your disposal."

"Snacks!" Kacey jumped up. She opened the mini refrigerator and started tossing bags at us.

"Potato chips!" she called out.

"Mine!" Isabel raised her hand and caught the bag one-handed.

"Pretzels!"

"Me, please!" Claire said. She caught the bag.

"Cheddar popcorn!" she yelled. Kacey tossed the bag of popcorn at me and ...

Woops! I missed! It flew right over my head and ...

WOP!

... bonked my mom right in the head.

chapter 4

My mom had walked into the room. And been hit by a bag of snacks!

"Whoops!" Kacey said. "I'm so sorry, Mrs. Sparks."

"Ack! Mom!" I said. "I totally missed!"

My mom was laughing.

"I was just coming in to say good night," she said. "I didn't realize this was dangerous territory."

"Good night everyone," mom said. Mom came over and gave me a hug and kiss goodnight. Then she leaned down and picked up the bag of popcorn. "And thanks for the nighttime snack!" She went back into her room

"Hey!" I yelled. "My mom just stole my snack!"

WOP!

"HEY!" I yelled again! I got hit in the head with something. A bag of cheese puffs!

Kacey was smiling all innocent.

"Just giving you a snack!" Kacey said.

I threw the bag right back at her.

"Food fight!" I yelled.

Lauren stuck her head in.

"Just kidding!" I told her. "Not a real food fight. The food's still in the bags. Just tossing bags. No mess."

Lauren just shook her head and disappeared back in her room.

"Lauren is way cool," I said.

"So's your mom," Kacey said. "I can't wait til my mom can travel with me."

Kacey's mom was pregnant! Way pregnant! Kacey was going to have a brand new baby sister or brother soon!

"Oh yeah! Maddy, you have to meet my grandma," Isabel said. She went over and knocked on one of the doors. Isabel's grandmother came in. She had dark hair like Isabel. She was kinda small but had a big smile on her face.

"Hey Gran, Maddy's here," Isabel said.

"Maddy, it's so nice to meet you," Isabel's grandmother said. She kissed my cheek. "The girls said very nice things about you on the plane."

"You know what else we talked about on the plane?" Kacey asked. "Gran was telling us some great stories about when Isabel was little."

"Yeah!" Isabel groaned. "Very embarrassing!"

I couldn't even imagine Isabel doing anything embarrassing. She was always so ... cool. And calm ... and confident.

Isabel's grandmother smiled. "I saved the juiciest ones for the flight back."

"Gran, noooo!" Isabel groaned. But she was laughing.

Gran said good night and went back to her room.

Everyone sat down on a bed, munching out. I started to unpack my stuff.

"Oh, you guys!" Claire said. "I almost forgot. I have a present for you."

Claire is way generous! She pulled out some t-shirts from her suitcase.

"You don't have to wear them if you don't want to," Claire said shyly. She handed them out.

Ohmigosh!

"These are sooo cute!" Kacey squealed. They totally were. They were white long-sleeve t-shirts with sparkly initials on them. Mine said M! For Maddy!!!!

"Turn them over," Claire said.

And on the back they said ...

TOOPALOOZA TOO CREW!

"These are so great. I can't wait to wear mine tomorrow," I told her. I gave her a hug. That was so nice!!!

"Oh, it wasn't anything much," Claire said.

"Claire!" Isabel and I said it at the same time: "Just say THANK YOU!"

"Thank you," Claire said, smiling.

"Maddy, you did miss something on the trip here," Kacey said. "Isabel taught us this new thing."

OK ...?

Isabel, Kacey, and Claire jumped up. They all started bumping fists, then slapping hands, then did a high five. And then they yelled woo hoo! And then they cracked up.

Oh. OK, they all had some "inside" move they were doing together. They all knew it. I didn't. I felt a little left out ...

For like one second! Because they all waved me over!

"Come on, Maddy!" Kacey said. "You have to learn this, too!"

I got up and tried it.

Fist, fist, hand slap, hand slap,
High-five, woo hoo!

Except I was like this ...

Fist, fist. Um, what's next? Wait, where does my hand go?!

"That's OK, let's try again," Isabel said.

Fist, fist, hand slap, hand slap ...

"Ow!" Kacey said, rubbing the side of her head.

"Sorry," I told her. "I meant to slap your hand!"

I felt totally stupid! I couldn't get it right!

"Forget it," I said. "I can't do it. Do it without me."

"It's OK, Maddy," Claire said. "We'll practice til you get it."

"It takes me forever to get the moves right," I said. "When you guys are high fiving, I'm slapping. Just forget it. With my luck, I'll probably give one of you a black eye!"

"No way, Maddy," Kacey said. "Let's just keep doing it til you get it."

"No! Face it! I'm a Hopeless SuperKlutz, OK?!?!" I yelled. "I'm the one who trips and falls in catazine shoots! And in class! And off the bus! And everywhere!! It's way frustrating, OK!?!"

"Maddy," Isabel said. "It's OK. You've got a baaaaad attitude. Come on ... real slow ..."

> *Fist, fist, hand slap, hand slap,*
> *High-five, woo hoo!*

We did it again! I screwed it up. And again! I screwed it up. And again! And then ...

I GOT IT! I did it!

"Alright, Maddy!" Everyone was cheering! Woo hoo!

"After we yell woo hoo," Isabel said. "We should yell something ... like ... TOO Crew!"

"Or TOO-Crew-Palooza!" I yelled.

We all cracked up!!!! OK! Again!

> *Fist, fist, hand slap, hand slap,*
> *High-five, woo hoo!*
> *TOO-Crew-Palooza!*

YAY!!!!

"I knew you could do it!" Isabel said.

"I'm so beat!" I said, flopping down on a bed. "That was hard work for a SuperKlutz like me."

"Yeah, we should probably get some sleep," Isabel said.

"Um, who's sleeping where?" I asked.

"Maddy, you're sharing a bed with me," Claire said. "Hope that's OK."

"I'm sharing with Kacey," Isabel said. "But I might end up on the floor."

"What are you talking about?" Kacey said.

"I'm thinking I'm going to get kicked and knocked off the bed! Because I can't imagine you ever staying still!" Isabel teased her. "Even when you sleep!"

We all looked at Kacey. Even now she was bouncing around on the bed! Isabel and Claire and I were lying around, but Kacey was like ... bounce! Bounce! Bounce!

"Oh yeah!" she said. "You're right! Better put some blankets on the floor, Isabel!"

We all laughed.

I opened my suitcase and got out my pajama pants. "Oh, shoot," I said. "I forgot a shirt to sleep in."

"No problemo!" Kacey jumped up. "You can borrow one of mine." She pulled out a t-shirt and flung it at me.

"Oh," I said, holding it up. "Thanks, but I don't think so." The shirt said "Property of Cheer Squad" on it.

"Why not?" said Isabel

"Well, you know. I'm not a cheerleader like you and Kacey," I mumbled.

"You don't have to be a cheerleader to wear it. It's just fun," Kacey said.

"Cheering isn't just rah rah for one sports team," Isabel said. "It's all about getting people psyched up for something! Spreading cheer! Like school spirit, too!"

"Besides, I'm not going to cheerlead this year," Kacey said. "But I'm keeping the shirt."

"You're not cheerleading?" I asked her. I couldn't imagine Kacey not making cheerleading. She was the captain last year! Plus, she was Super Spirited!

"Nope, I didn't even try out," Kacey said. "'Cuz my soccer schedule was too crazy this year. I liked cheerleading, but it wasn't as major as soccer for me. And I don't want to overload. After soccer, I'll do basketball ... oh also, volleyball, track in the spring and ...."

Kacey is seriously sporty!!!

"That reminds me," Isabel said. "Aren't your cheerleading tryouts coming up soon, Maddy?"

"That's right!" Claire said to me. "Are you going to try out?"

"Um, yeah," I said. "I am. Well, I signed up, anyway."

"Awesome!" Isabel said.

"You really want to make it, don't you?" said Claire. "Because all your friends are doing it, right?"

"Yeah," I said, sitting down next to her on the bed. "That's one reason. But also ... I just really like cheerleading. This summer I practiced cheerleading with my friends all the time, you know? And I was realizing ... I guess I miss it."

"I know what you mean," Claire said. "I really missed not playing violin in orchestra all summer. I had to practice by myself."

"ACK!" Kacey screamed. "Violin! Yikes!"

We all laughed.

"Well, I'll stick to violin. You stick to basketball," Claire said to Kacey. "That's MY Yikes!"

"How's your practice going now?" Isabel asked me.

"Oh. Uh," I said. "I haven't really been practicing. I mean, a little bit in my room. But every time I start to practice I stop."

"What happens?" Claire asked.

"I can't stop thinking: I STINK!" I blurted out. "I mean, I didn't make it the first time. So every time I get up to do a cheer I'm thinking about how bad I am. That I'm stupid for trying out again."

"Well!" Isabel stood up. "We're going to do something about that! You can't try out again without practicing."

"I know," I said miserably.

"Show us your cheer!" Kacey said. "Show us what you did for tryouts last time."

"I can't do that!" I said. Way too embarrassing! I can't just get up and do that.

"No, really," Isabel said. "I helped judge cheer tryouts this season. I learned a lot about what the judges are looking for."

"That's OK," I said. "Forget it."

Isabel wasn't about to.

"What do you think you did wrong the first time?" she asked.

"Was it your jumps? Was it your chants? Weren't you spirited enough? What do you think you need to work on?"

Um ...

"Did you ask the coach what you can do to improve? Have you asked anyone for help?"

"Um, no ..." I said. "Brittany did tell me a couple things ...."

"Phht! Brittany!" Kacey said. "She probably told you wrong things on purpose. Just to screw you up!"

They all had met Brittany at the *TOO's U-Pick Challenge* Contest. She was ... well, not showing her better side there. She used to have a better side! She used to be fun! Silly! Crazy! But I hadn't seen her good side much lately!

"It's late. We shouldn't be too loud," I said.

Everyone just looked at me.

"Oh, ALL right," I sighed. I got up and went over to the corner of the room where there was space.

"Do it exactly as you remember doing it when you tried out," said Isabel. "Pretend I'm really a judge. Ready ...?"

"OK!" I cheered. "Green and white! Let's go and fight ..."

When I finished I ran over and jumped on the bed. Then I pulled the covers over my head. I felt so stupid!

Isabel, Kacey, and Claire clapped for me.

"OK, I know I stunk," I said, still hiding under the blankets. "Thanks for not laughing at me."

"OK, Maddy, guess what. You totally don't stink," said Kacey.

"She's right," said Isabel. "You don't stink. Could you be better? Sure."

Well, OK. At least I didn't TOTALLY stink.

"Now," Isabel continued. "Do you realllllly want to make cheerleading?"

"Yeah," I said, from under the covers. "I really do."

"'Cuz I think I can help you out," Isabel said. "I have some ideas if you want to hear them."

I peeked out. Kacey and Claire were sitting there, listening.

They weren't laughing. They weren't looking at each other

like, "Poor Maddy thinks she has a chance? Ha!" They weren't rolling their eyes like, "Oh puh-lease. What is Maddy thinking?"

"Maddy, I can help you, too!" Kacey said.

"I don't know cheerleading, but I know dance," Claire said.

"Ummmmmm," I said. "OK! Tell me what I should do."

OK. I was ready. Tell me what stupid things I do.

Kacey spoke first.

"My big thing that I saw was ... well. You say you like to cheer. But you didn't really look like it! You weren't smiling! You were acting like we forced you to be up there!"

"Well I sorta was!" I grumbled.

"I know," said Isabel, all reassuring me. "It's totally nervous to be up there. But you gotta get used to it. Hey, Kacey, you're awesome at being smiley. Maybe you can be in charge of pumping Maddy up for spirit."

"Sure!" Kacey said.

Well, that was true! I could definitely take spirit lessons from Kacey! Who couldn't?!!

"Actually, Maddy," Isabel said. "I thought your arm motions were awesome. But your jumps weren't as tight as you might want them to be. I can help you work on that!"

"OK, this sounds silly ...." Claire said. "But I had to take this class on being graceful. My father made me. I could help you with that."

I felt my face get all hot. They were all looking at me!

"Maddy!" said Isabel. "I know we all have suggestions. But you're pretty close! I think you can do this!"

"You do?" I asked. I looked at everyone. You know what? If Kacey could help me be peppier. If Isabel could help me with the jumps and tumbling. If Claire could help me be, well, not so klutzy .... Hm ...!

"You guys really want to help me?" I asked them, shyly.

"YEAH!" they all said.

"When we get back from Toopalooza, we will have TOO Crew School of Cheerleading Tryouts!" Isabel said.

"Go, Maddy!" Kacey cheered. "Go, Maddy, go!"

Knock, knock! A door opened. Lauren stuck her head in.

"Ahem," she said. "Go Maddy go is right. Go Maddy go to Bed! Go Kacey, Go Isabel, and Go Claire ... to sleep!!!"

Oopsie!

"That was very motivating," Claire said to Lauren, seriously. "You would make a good cheerleader, Lauren."

We all busted out laughing.

"SLEEP, girls!" Lauren said. But she was smiling.

"We will!" we said.

And this time, when Kacey tossed me her extra shirt ... I put it on.

chapter 5

"Riiiiiiiiiiiiiing!"

Mmmf. Time to get up for school. Not in the mood for school. Nope. I felt around to hit the snooze button.

"Ow!"

That was no alarm clock! I opened my eyes quick. I'd just ...

"You just poked me in the eye!" Claire said, sleepily.

"Ohmigosh I'm sorry, Claire!" I said.

"I'm fine," Claire said. "Don't worry!"

"You're fine," Isabel said. "You're not the one who got karate kicked by Kacey all night."

"Oh!" Kacey said, sitting up. "Sorry! I was dreaming about soccer! I was winning the World Cup and ... AHHHHHHHH!"

Kacey JUMPED out of bed!

"Do you guys realize what day this is?!?!" she screamed. "IT'S TOOPALOOZA DAY!!!!!!"

No snooze button for me! I was going to Toopalooza! I jumped out of bed.

"Ohmigosh! I wonder what we're going to be doing today!" I said.

Knock! Knock! The door opened. And Lauren came in.

"Good morning, girls!" Lauren said. "Anyone interested in what you'll be doing today?"

Yeah! Yeah! Yeah and Yeah!

This is what Lauren told us:

- ☆ Our first assignment would be off and on all day.
- ☆ We would have a videocamera.
- ☆ We should film anything we wanted to at Toopalooza.
    What we do!
    What we see!
    What we like!
    Who we talk to!
- ☆ We will get to go behind the scenes with the camera.
- ☆ And make a "documentary" of Toopalooza! Too coool!

"This will help our Limited Too executives see the music fest through the eyes of our most important concert-goers—you girls," Lauren said. "I want you to just tell us what you see and how you feel about it. So, here's a little camera 101 ... gather round girls."

She showed us the buttons. Then she handed it to me.

"Testing, testing," I said. *"Introducing the Too-Crew-Palooza girls ... There's Isabel ..."*

"Hey!" Isabel laughed. "Get that thing off me! Wait til I take a shower!" She went to get ready.

"Film me! Film me!" Kacey said, jumping on one of the beds.

"Scratch that. Here's Kacey," I said. I pressed Record. Kacey bounced! And jumped! And did splits!

"OK," I said. "Let's make sure that worked."

I hit rewind and then play. We heard my voice, "Testing, testing. Introducing the Too-Crew-Palooza TOO Crew ... There's Isabel."

Claire and I peeked through the viewer. All I saw was a big thumb.

"Maybe try moving your finger off the lens," Claire suggested.

"Oops," I said.

Take 2!

Isabel walked out in a robe with her towel on her head.

"Here comes future fashion designer Isabel, modeling her latest creation ..." I announced, turning the camera at her.

"Hey!" Isabel laughed. "Get that thing off me!"

"Don't worry," Kacey said. "Maddy's filming. You'll just see a big giant thumb."

"Hmph," I said, rewinding and looking at it. "I was about to feel insulted. But you're right, I did it again! I better get the hang of this. Or the documentary will be called Thumb-a-Palooza."

Even Lauren cracked up!

"Nope," I said. "I'm going to lose the thumb. Our videotape is Tape-a-Palooza. And I'll figure it out."

Then the video camera went Whhhhhhhhhhhrp!

Or maybe not. That didn't sound so good.

"Um, maybe someone else wants to do the camera?" I asked.

"Let me try it," Claire said. "I'll film you, Maddy."

"Hey, Mad, do your cheer," Isabel said. "Then you can take a look at what you look like doing it."

ACK!

"Isn't it bad enough you guys saw my humiliation?" I groaned.

"No, tape it. That's a good way to see what you're really doing," Isabel said. "We'll delete it later."

Oh, OK. I did my cheer. Got it over with.

Then Claire rewound the videocamera. And I peeked through it.

There I was ... bouncing, cheering, and ...

"Oh nooo," I said. Oh no! Isabel was right. I could see something I was doing wrong.

My arms were OK. My moves were OK. My jumps weren't great, but I knew that. But my face ...

My face looked like ... ACKKKKKKKKK!

"Ackkkkk!" I screamed. "I thought I was smiling!"

I was sooo not smiling when I was doing that cheer. There was sooo not a smile on my face. There was a look on my face like ...

Stressed out!

"I look like I'm in pain!" I groaned. "I'm soooo not smiling!"

Hel-lo! Cheerleaders have to smile!!!! The judges were probably like, um, this girl is so not smiley. Buh-bye.

"Welp," Isabel said cheerfully. "Now you know one thing to work on. We have to practice your smiling when you cheer."

I hit rewind. I wanted that deleted fast! I would have to force myself to smile during tryouts if it killed me!

"Girls!" Lauren called out. "Heads up! We'll be leaving soon!"

Yup, it was my turn to get ready for ....

TOOPALOOZA!

And I knew I wouldn't have to force myself to smile for that!!!

I checked myself out in the mirror. Was I ready for Toopalooza?

☆ Hair: Looking good thanks to Isabel! She put my hair in two low ponytails.

☆ Face: Regular me, with new peachy lip gloss, yum!

☆ Jewelry: My charm bracelet! And a silvery choker!

☆ Clothes: Denim skorts, my Reeboks ... and ...

☆ My Toopalooza TOO Crew "M" t-shirt!

"Hey, we're looking good," Isabel said. "We should be catazine models!" Hee!

Kacey was wearing her "K" t-shirt with pedals and sneakers. Instead of her usual ponytails, Isabel had done her hair in little twists on the side of her head.

Isabel was wearing her "I" t-shirt with cargoes and boots. Her hair was up under a cool hat. Claire was wearing her "C" t-shirt with a pleated skirt and buckle shoes. Isabel had done Claire's hair, too. It was in two long braids.

"Are you ready, girls?" my mom called in. "Lauren and Isabel's grandmother are getting the elevator."

WE WERE READY!!!

Fist, fist, hand slap, hand slap,
High-five, woo hoo!

We all yelled it ... TOO-CREW-PALOOZA!!!!

* * * * * * *

In the taxi, Lauren told us a little more about what we were going to do.

"You are going to be runners for two music acts," she told us.

"What's a runner?" I asked.

"A runner is someone who helps out the musicians with anything they might need," Lauren explained. "Of course, they have many people to help them prepare. You'll see how it all works. But we need runners to help them with errands and things they might need somebody. Like a go-fer."

And first, we would be runners for Nina Miles.

"Nina Miles is going to be here?" I asked.

We knew who she was! We had seen her video in *TOO's U-Pick Challenge* Contest! She was this super singer and dancer. And really bouncy, just like Kacey!

"Yes, she just signed with a new music label involved in Toopalooza," Lauren said. "So she's going to perform a song."

"Nina Miles was my fave at *TOO's U-Pick Challenge!*" Kacey squealed. "That's so cool!"

"I remember that," Lauren smiled. "So Kacey, I'm putting you in charge of that job. You'll all work together, but you'll be the main person on it."

And then she told us that after we helped Nina, we would be runners for ... INSPIRE!

"Yay!" we all said.

"It was Alexa's special request," Lauren smiled. Alexa was the main singer in INSPIRE. We had first met her at a catazine shoot. She was sooo nice. And now she was in a band playing today!

"Isabel, I'm going to put you in charge of that job."

"But, Maddy was the one who really was into INSPIRE," Claire said. "Shouldn't she be in charge?"

"Oh, don't worry. I've got the perfect job for Maddy," Lauren said. "First, Claire, will be in charge of filming Toopalooza. You did a great job working the camera, I noticed. And Maddy, I'd like you to be the host of the video."

"ME?" I squeaked.

"Yes," said Lauren. "Ever since I saw you in Hollywood hosting your pretend TOO Crew Awards, I thought you would be a great interviewer."

Oh! When we were in the restaurant about to meet Jennifer, the Grand Prize Winner of the Zoe Zone contest.

"Yeah, I remember that!" said Kacey. "You were pretending to interview me, Isabel and Claire. You were so funny that Claire had to lie down on the stairs because she was laughing so hard."

"Ohmigosh, I remember," Claire said. "You'll be great Maddy!"

Me?

Me!

I'm going to be ... the official host of ...

TAPE-A-PALOOZA!

chapter 6

"*Reporting Live from LEGOLAND California®, it's the TOO Crew. I'm Maddy, your host today. And this is Kacey, Isabel, and Claire. We're standing in front of the site of the totally exciting Toopalooza. And we can't wait to get in there!!!!*"

We all went like AHHHHHHHHHHHHH!

"Cut!" Lauren said, giving Claire the camera. "Great start, girls. Claire, the camera is now officially yours."

"*Let's get our first look at LEGOLAND California. It's looking pretty amazing ... check out the banners. They're everywhere! They say, Toopalooza!*"

"Where do we go?" Kacey asked.

"Follow the daisies," Lauren said, pointing down. There were giant painted daisies making a path on the ground. "They lead to the table where we need to get your badges. And then they lead to the concert area."

We saw more banners that said Toopalooza on them. We walked through the turnstiles. We walked past shops and food places.

We got out our tickets to LEGOLAND. We went up to a table and Lauren gave our names.

We got a badge in a plastic holder. I slipped the lanyard over my neck. It looked like they were backstage passes ... very cool!

OK, excuse me, yes! I, Maddy Elizabeth Sparks, am wearing a badge. This badge that says ...

TOOPALOOZA

And the names of all the music acts appearing today! It also had a bunch of little outlines on it. Lauren said we'd be getting those punched when we went to a special area for girls to have fun when they're not at the concert.

That's what the real live passes say for all the girls who get to see the show! And ours also says ... CREW! Because we're part of the working crew today!

SWWWWWWWEEEEEET!!!

"Are you guys ready to work?" Mom asked.

Yes! Even work sounded fun ... if it was at a Toopalooza! With Kacey, Isabel, and Claire!

"Now we're walking through the park, toward the area where Toopalooza is going to be. There are LEGO® models everywhere! But not the kind of LEGO towers my brother Zack makes. They're like little worlds with moving parts and LEGO cars driving around.

Hey! Is that New York City made out of LEGO bricks? Totally wild. OK, let's go check it out!"

"Look!" Kacey pointed. "Check out the rollercoaster! I'm so there, later!"

"We've got some work to do before you guys explore the park," Lauren said. "First, you'll be runners for the music acts as they get ready for the show. Oh – and you can't film that part. You can start filming again later when you're done being runners."

"What's over there?" I pointed to where a bunch of people were setting up tents and tables and things.

"That's TOO-U!" Lauren pointed. "It's a really cool area of the event. Our Toopalooza audience will get to do a lot of really fun things over there, along with attending the concert. Like listen to hot new music at one pavillion, learn dance steps at another, do fashion games at another. You girls will be able to check that out and film there as well later."

We walked up to a big brown door.

"Behind the door is where the concert will be starting in just a few hours!" Lauren said.

The brown door didn't look like anything much. But through

it would be ... Toopalooza!!!!

"Chaperones, this is where we split up," Lauren said. "Pam, Mrs. Vega, Bruno ... enjoy the park and the Very Important Parents waiting area. I'll take good care of the girls of course. They'll have walkie-talkies."

"And yes, Bruno, I have my cell phone on," Claire said.

"If you need anything, my cell will be on," Mom said, giving me a hug. "I'm going to go see the sights with Isabel's grandmother. You have a wonderful time, sweetie."

Lauren went to a table and brought over walkie-talkies.

"We each get one," she said. "Just attach them to your pockets. We'll all be able to talk to each other no matter where we are in the park. And the talent you're helping also will have a walkie-talkie so they can buzz you."

I hit the button.

"Testing," I said.

Kwwwwrk!

Our walkie-talkies crackled.

"Testing!" we heard over all our walkie-talkies!

"THIS IS MADDY," I said into the walkie-talkie. *"CALLING ALL TOO-CREW-PALOOZA."*

Kwwwwrk! My voice came over loud. Whoops! Way loud!

"We read you," Isabel said back into hers. *"Loud and clear. Too loud!"*

We all cracked up.

And Lauren pushed the big brown door open ... and ...
This was it!!! I looked around.

We were on a really big lawn. In a few hours there would thousands of girls out there! And there was a stage! In a couple hours ... famous singers would be up there!

There were tons of people working all over the place. People setting up stuff on stage! People setting up stuff around the lawn! Lights! Microphones! Speakers!

"There's a lot to set up," Claire said. "Wow!"

"Sound checks are about to start," Lauren said.

"What's a sound check?" I asked.

"It's when a singer or music group comes onstage to test the stage and equipment," Lauren explained. "They practice a few songs and dances. And good timing to ask because look over there ..."

"Ohmigosh!!! That's PLAY!" I said.

chapter 7

The four singers in Play were walking out onto the stage! Practically right in front of us!!! They got in their places and ...

They started singing! Then they stopped. Then someone fixed their microphones or something. Then they did part of a dance. Then they stopped. Then they started singing more seriously and ...

AHHHHHHHH! I was standing here watching Play practice for the concert!

"They sound really good," Claire whispered to me. We watched them finish a song. There was this woman with super long hair giving them instructions on what to do. Sorta like being a director or something. Now that could be a cool job!

How cool was that?!?!

"And that was a sound check," Lauren said. "Now I'll show you other places you need to know."

OK! Here were the other places that the Crew had to know about:

Hospitality Tent: This was a fancy tent that would be a hangout for some people, who were part of the show and stuff. They could eat back there. It would be where the singers would go to meet people who were going to interview them. Like, TV people, radio people, magazine people. Like girls with a video camera making a behind the scenes movie ... ahem!!! (That's me!)

The Catering Tent: The place where the food was cooked and made. So if one of our stars asked for food, we'd go here and get it for them. (And we would get to eat lunch there, too! Yum!)

The Trailers: All of the singers stay in hotels overnight. And then they have trailers parked out back where they get ready today and stay while the concert is going on.

We had to show our badges to go to the trailer area. Because it was closed to everyone who wasn't working with the singers! But the TOO Crew could go in!!!

There were a bunch of trailers parked all over the ground. We passed a trailer that had a sign on it:

Mandy Moore

"Ohmigosh," I said. "Mandy Moore could be in there right now." We stopped and stared at it.

We passed a trailer that said:

Jessica Simpson

OK, hel-lo? Was this all really happening!!! Or am I just dreaming like the best dream in my whole life?!

"Now girls," Lauren said. "Just remember, before a show singers are very busy. They might be nervous and even stressed. So your job is just to be there to help them so they can concentrate on their performance."

OK! I can do that! Whatever Nina wants! I can do it!

Lauren went up to one of the talent trailers and knocked. The door opened and a woman stuck her head out.

"Hi, Felicia," Lauren said. "The runners are here." Felicia is Nina's manager.

We all went in.

"Nina's in the changing area," Felicia said.

I looked around the trailer. It looked like a tiny house on wheels! There was a little kitchen with a sink and fridge. There was a sofa with a table. I saw a TV and a stereo system built in. It looked like a bathroom and a closet off to the side. A big mirror was on the wall. There was a big screen *thingy*. That must be the changing area.

And it was so bright! Lights everywhere! Big light bulbs! I bet that's for when she has to get ready. I remembered all the lights from when we did makeup, hair, and wardrobe at the catazine photo shoot. It looked kinda like that.

And then from behind the screen, came Nina Miles! I recognized Nina Miles from her video. She was wearing track pants and a tank top. She wasn't wearing any makeup, and her hair was up in a towel. She looked at us.

"This is Maddy, Kacey, Isabel, and Claire," Lauren said. "They'll be here to help you out."

"OK," Nina said.

"I have to go take care of a few things," Lauren said. "Just page me on the walkie-talkie if you need anything, OK?"

OK!

Lauren left the trailer. And Kacey, Isabel, Claire and I ... stood there. OK! Now what?

"Um, can we help you?" I asked Nina, as she was toweling off her hair.

"Here's the sitch, Isabel," Nina said to me. "I'll talk, you listen."

"Um, actually I'm Maddy and I'm happy to-" I started to say.

But she cut me off.

"Look, if you have something to say, say it to my manager. She can tell me if it's important. I'm going to call you One. The girl with the pigtails is Two. Hat girl you're Three. Blondie, you're Four. OK, I'm starving. I need breakfast."

And with that, Nina turned around and walked away.

One, Two, Three, and Four looked at each other. We climbed out of the trailer.

"Ooookay," I said. "Is it me or were we just totally blown off?"

chapter 8

"Well, we're here to work," Isabel said. "So we've just got to deal. We've got to do what it takes for Nina to be ready for the show."

So we went to get ...

Breakfast!

We all ran over to the catering tent. There was a cook cooking away.

"Hi," Isabel said. "Breakfast for one of the performers, please."

"What would she like?" the chef asked. "Eggs? Pancakes? French toast?"

We all looked at each other. Isabel shrugged. Nina had walked away before we could ask! We thought maybe there was just one choice!

"Um, what do they usually like?" I asked.

The chef laughed. "Every performer likes different things. How about I make you an assortment?"

"Thank you," said Claire. He gave us each a plate of food.

"Wow, four different breakfasts," I said.

We knocked on the trailer. Felicia stuck her head out.

"We're not sure what Nina wants, so we brought choices," Claire said.

"Nina!" Felicia called out. "Breakfast is here!" She motioned for us to come in so we did.

"What's that?" Nina asked.

"Scrambled eggs and toast," I said.

"That is so not what I wanted!" Nina said. "What else is there? Number 2?"

"Waffles! And fruit cup!" Kacey said.

"Oh, puh-lease!" she said. "Number 3?"

"Pancakes and bacon," Isabel said.

"Not," Nina said. "Number 4?"

"French toast and sausage?" Claire tried.

"No, no, and no way! I want an omelet with green—not red—

peppers and toast and orange juice! Yeesh! Don't you people know anything?"

Ooookay.

"Do you want this toast for now?" I asked her.

"That toast has butter on it," Nina said. "I need mine no butter and slightly burnt around the edges. No jelly on the plate. Hurry before I pass out from hunger."

And she turned around.

Ooooooooooooooooooooookay.

"That's sooo not what I asked for," Kacey mimicked under her breath. "That's soooo not what I thought she'd be like. I'm glad she didn't win the *TOO's U-Pick Challenge* Contest!"

"Easy," Isabel said, calmly. "It's our job to make this go smoothly. So let's just get her food." We headed over to the catering tent.

"Did the breakfast choices work, girls?" the chef asked. Then he looked at the plates we were still carrying. "Perhaps not."

"May we please have an omelet with green peppers and toast with no butter, slightly burned," Kacey asked.

"While I cook that up, feel free to eat the other food I made," the chef said. "No sense in letting good food go to waste."

We all looked at each other. We were supposed to get a breakfast break. I was hungry. "I wouldn't mind a pancake."

We all sat down and scarfed down the food. Yum!

Kwwwwrk! Our walkie-talkies went off.

"One! Two! Three! Four! I'm faint from hunger. Bring my food!"

Oh nooooo! It was Nina!

"Hurry!" Kacey said.

"Almost done," the chef said. "Just burning the toast ... and here ..."

Kacey grabbed the plate and we took off to Nina's trailer.

Kwwwwrk! "One, two, three and four? Where are you?"

"We're coming!" Kacey yelled, running.

"Nina says to come in," Felicia said when we got there.

Nina was getting her makeup done. She didn't even turn

around.

"Tea," commanded Nina. "Raspberry tea with lemon. And a side of honey. For my voice."

We headed back outside.

"What happened to 'Thank you for getting me breakfast?'" Kacey said. "Or at least a hello? Augh."

"I know," Isabel said. "What a diva. OK, we have to get tea. Let's hit the catering tent again."

Kwwwwrk! "One, Two, Three and Four! Don't let the tea be too hot! Or too cold!"

"Let's go!" We started running.

"Help!" Kacey said to the chef. "Our singer wants raspberry tea with lemon and honey on the side!"

"I've got regular, mint, cinnamon, ginger, and green tea," the chef said.

Claire turned on her walkie-talkie.

"Hi, Nina? There's regular, mint tea, cinnamon, and green tea," she said into it.

Kwwwwrk! "I said raspberry tea. And hurry up!"

"Sorry," the chef said. "You might try the hospitality tent."

"OK, let's split up and cover everything," Isabel said. "Maddy, you hit the hospitality tent. Claire, how about you try to find Lauren. Kacey, we can check out the shops at the entrance of the park. Report in on your walkie-talkie if you find it."

We all took off. I ran to the hospitality tent.

Raspberry tea. Raspberry tea. OK! Must find raspberry tea! Whew! This was seriously hard work being a runner! Especially for Nina Miles. I was getting kinda hot! Kinda sweaty! But I could do it!

I ran over into the hospitality tent ... and ....

BAM!

I ran smack into a girl carrying her breakfast! I ran right into her plate of food! Oh no! Waffles and whipped cream ... right in my face!!!!

Red-face Rating: ★★★ out of ★★★★★ stars.
Well, you couldn't tell I had a red face! It was covered in white whipped cream!!!!

"I can't believe you did that!" the girl said.

Wait a minute ... I knew that voice. I wiped the whipped cream out of my eyes so I could see.

It was ... PIPER.

Piper! What was Piper doing here?

"Um, sorry," I said.

"Lucky for you, you didn't ruin my new shirt," Piper said. Then she looked up. "Hey! It's you! Figures. You knock everyone over at the catazine shoot, now you knock my breakfast over. You're just going to have to get me a new breakfast."

AUGH! I can't believe this is happening!

"Anyway, what are you doing here?" Piper asked.

"The TOO Crew is helping with Toopalooza," I said. "Are you here working, too?"

"Working?" Piper said, waving her hand in the air. "Puh-lease. I don't think so. I'm here as a special invited guest. With my dad. He is very connected in the music industry, you know."

Kwwwwrk! "An extra lemon slice. I need an extra lemon slice."

"Um, that's Nina Miles," I said. "We're helping her out."

"After you get my waffles, right?" Piper said.

"Uh, I guess so but I'm in a big hurry and—"

"I'll wait here. Then I have a busy day. Hanging out here with important people. Riding some rides," Piper said.

Kwwwwrk! "Guys, It's Isabel. No luck here with Claire or Kacey. How 'bout you, Maddy?"

Ack! I have to find raspberry tea! I gotta hurry!

"Look! Entertainment at Night is here filming!" Piper said. "Forget breakfast. I better get over there. Maybe I'll be asked to do some interviews. I am the Taco Tiko Princess you know."

Oh yeah. I knew. Mmmmm burritos and all that.

"How's my hair look? I'm sure it looks great," Piper was saying. As I took off!

Kwwwwrk! "And a fresh teaspoon! Make sure there are no spots!"

NINA!

"I'm coming!" I said into the walkie-talkie, as nice as I could.

Considering I had Piper in my face! Nina in my face! Whipped cream all over my face!!!

I looked around the hospitality tent. I found an area with tea ... lemon tea, cinnamon tea ... please please have ... YES!!!

RASPBERRY TEA!!! WOO HOOO!!!!!!

"Got it!" I yelled into the walkie-talkie. *"Meet you guys back at the trailer!"* I ran to the trailer. As fast as I could. With a cup of warm not hot or cold tea and lemon and a cup of honey and a fresh teaspoon!

I ran back to Nina's trailer. I bumped into Kacey, Isabel, and Claire heading that way, too.

"Yay, Maddy!" Kacey said. "Maddy saves the day!"

"Did you have to run through whipped cream to get it?" Isabel asked me.

Huh? Oh yeah.

"Ugh, I totally didn't have a chance to clean up," I said. "Long story. But listen to this. You're not going to believe who I just saw in the Hospitality Tent."

"Nick Cannon? Ashlee Simpson?" Kacey squealed.

"No, it's so not even a good thing," I said. "PIPER is here!"

Everybody groaned.

Kwwwwrk!

We all grabbed our walkie-talkies and hit the button at the same time.

"WE'RE COMING!!!!"

chapter 9

"Raspberry tea! With lemon and a side of honey! And a fresh teaspoon!" I placed everything down in front of Nina.

Nina frowned.

"Raspberry tea? I said wild berry tea," Nina said.

"Oh, excuse us, but you did say raspberry tea," Claire spoke up politely and nicely.

"Did I say that? Well I really want wild berry." Nina said.

I looked at the TOO Crew.

ARGH!

"Don't say anything," Isabel whispered. "Let's just go."

We walked out.

"That girl!" Kacey said. "Can you imagine!"

"Let's just get her the tea," Isabel said.

"I think I saw some at the hospitality tent," I told everyone.

So we ran back to the hospitality tent and got some wild berry tea. Then we ran back to Nina's trailer.

Kacey was really kinda mad!

"I'm taking back my vote on *TOO's U-Pick Challenge*," she said. "If Nina Miles' video comes on TV, I'm changing channels!"

"Take a deep breath," Isabel said to Kacey. "Relax. We'll go in and get this over with."

We knocked on the trailer and went in.

"Here's your wild berry tea–" I said and stopped. Because sitting next to Nina Miles in her trailer was ... Piper.

"Hiiiiii workers," said Piper, all sticky sweet. "Working hard?"

Bluch! Ick! Yuk!

"Hello, Piper," Claire said politely.

"What are you doing here?" Kacey asked.

"My dad has tons of connections. Not only to see the show. But to visit some celebrities. Like Nina Miles, my fave singer in the whole world always," Piper said.

Nina smiled at her.

Oh puh-lease! When we were watching videos for the *TOO's U-Pick Challenge* Contest, Piper had said something like, "Compared to POSE, Nina Miles has no talent."

Now she's sucking up.

"While you're here, girls," Piper said. "I'd like some chamomile tea. With lemon."

We looked at each other. I mean, we're not working for Piper ...

"You heard my biggest fan," said Nina. "Go get some chamomile tea. With lemon."

AUGH!! We have to be runners for ... Piper? Ugh, ugh, and ugh-ly!

"Hel-looo?" Piper said. "Nina just told you girls to get my–"

But just then ...

Kwwwwrk!

"TOO Crew!" It was Lauren. *"I let Felicia know that you need to move on to your next assignment. Meet me outside!"*

YAY! Lauren saves the day.

"Oh, so sorry," Isabel said. "Sorry, Piper. Must run."

And we RAN out of there!!! FAST!!

We ran over to where Lauren was waiting for us.

"OK, girls," Lauren said. "How was your first assignment? And Maddy, you've got a little bit of white something on your cheek, there. And, er, in your hair ..."

We all looked at each other.

"We'll fill you in later," Isabel said.

"We can't wait to hear what's next!" I said, wiping my cheek.

"Good attitude," Lauren said. "Next up, you'll be runners for INSPIRE. We still have a few hours before the show's going to begin. So you'll help out INSPIRE for a little while and then we'll get you started filming the event."

Cool!

It was time to be runners again ... for INSPIRE!

I was feeling nervous! Nina was running us everywhere! What if INSPIRE was like that? What if even Alexa turned into a diva? Now that they were getting famous, I guess you never know!

We all went over to INSPIRE's trailer. KNOCK! KNOCK!

Lauren knocked on another trailer. A woman poked her head out.

"Hi, you ready for your runners?" Lauren asked.

"Absolutely," the woman said. "I'm INSPIRE's manager, Val. Come on in."

We walked in. I didn't say anything. I didn't want to talk again when I wasn't supposed to!!!

"Yay!" Alexa said, running over. "I'm so glad you guys are here!"

OK! This was a better start than Nina Miles! Alexa introduced everyone.

Eden! With the long straight black hair. Morgan! With the brown short hair with red streaks in it. Sabrina! With the short blonde crimpy hair. And Alexa, of course, with the long blondish brown hair with bangs.

They all said, "HI!" And didn't tell us not to talk unless they talked to us first!

"NICE shirts!" Morgan said, looking at our t-shirts.

"You guys looked great in the catazine!" Alexa said. We told her she did, too!

"I hear you guys did an awesome job at lip synching like us at the *TOO's U-Pick Challenge* Contest," Eden said.

"I was YOU, Eden!" Kacey said to her. Kacey did a couple of Eden's dance moves. Everyone cracked up.

"But really, thanks sooo much for helping to make us *TOO's U-Pick Challenge* winners," Sabrina said in a quiet voice.

"We can't wait to do the show today!" Morgan said. "But we've got a lot to do to get ready. Sit down and hang out until our manager gets back. We're not going onstage til later in the show."

"So you guys want to show us your lip synch?" Alexa asked. "The one you did at *TOO's U-Pick Challenge* Contest?"

"Really? You want to see it? OK!" Kacey said. She jumped up. So did Isabel. Even Claire stood up. But not me. This could be embarrassing! I wasn't good at getting up and doing stuff in front of people. I was always way nervous! Way embarrassed! And to do it in front of an about-to-be-famous band?

Um ...

"Come on, Maddy," Alexa said. "Don't be embarrassed. Show us your winning moves."

"Well, that's kind of the thing," I said. "I don't really have any moves. Which, um, if we did your song right now you would see for yourself. Isabel, Kacey, Claire ... all good dancers. Me, nope."

"Maddy isn't confident about her dancing," Isabel said.

"So I did a lot of guitar action," I told them. "Just pretending to sing and play while everyone else danced."

All of a sudden INSPIRE started cracking up laughing.

"What?" I asked. Did I say something funny?

"Maddy, not being a great dancer is nothing to be embarrassed about," Alexa said. "Everyone can't be a great dancer. I totally relate!"

"But you're onstage dancing and singing and stuff!" I said.

"Yes, but I'm not as good as Eden, Morgan, or Sabrina," Alexa said. "That's why you see me playing my guitar in the major complicated dance scenes! I can't do all the moves."

"But whoa, can that girl sing!" Morgan said.

"Alexa rocks on her guitar, too," Eden said.

"Thanks," Alexa said. "But yeah, I'm not as good a dancer. I'm practicing, though!"

"Yeah," I said. "Maybe I need to practice more. You guys must practice dancing all the time."

Then INSPIRE started cracking up again.

"What did I say?!?!" I asked.

"I practice dancing all the time," Alexa said. "Sabrina and Morgan practice all the time, too. Eden ... she doesn't practice so much."

"Because Eden doesn't need to practice as much," Sabrina said. "Eden has natural talent like you wouldn't believe. She can practically jump into any routine and BAM! She has it down."

"Well, my parents told me I was born dancing," Eden said. "Dancing just seems to come naturally to me."

"We all have our different things we're better at," Alexa said. "And our things we're not so good at. But when we put them together ... it seems to work!"

"So come on," Morgan said. "Nobody's gonna make fun of your dancing, Maddy. Can we see the routine?"

"Here," Sabrina said and handed me a guitar. "Hide behind this."

"OK," Isabel said to me. "Want to show them our routine?"

Oh, okay. They were so nice! I couldn't say no! We all got up.

"Can we get some music?" Kacey asked. "Your *Looking Up* song? Do you have a CD player in here?"

"Hey, we need to stretch our voices for the show," said Sabrina.

And Sabrina started to sing ...

Think you're facing ... the world all alone?
It's all going by without you ...

Then Morgan ...

Think that things will never be good again?

Then Alexa!

You think you're alone, girl?

Just listen to this song, girl!
And see that's all so wrong, girl ... 'cuz ...

INSPIRE was singing right there for us! Singing *Looking Up!*
The song I first heard on the radio when I was all bummed
out. And it cheered me up.

IT GAVE ME CHILLS!

I got a huge smile on my face. And the TOO Crew started doing
their dance from the *TOO's U-Pick Challenge* Contest.

- ★ Step 1 and 2
- ★ Cross turn
- ★ Clap left twice and right turn
- ★ Step kick
- ★ Push back
- ★ Step 7 and 8

Kacey, Isabel, and Claire were dancing! I was jamming on the
guitar! And smiling! I can't believe my new favorite group was
singing a mini-concert right in front of me!

Because ... things are LOOKING UP!
Yeah, things are looking up!
Things couldn't be looking any better!

And one ... two ... three ... DONE!

Woo hoo!!!!!!!

INSPIRE started clapping for us! And we were clapping for them!

"That was awesome you guys!" Morgan said.

"No YOU guys were awesome!" Isabel said back.

That. Was. Very.

COOL!!!!!!!

"You sounded great," Claire said.

"I hope we sound great for Toopalooza!" Eden said.

"We're sooo nervous!" Sabrina said. "This is so huge for us!"

"We did our sound check," Alexa said. "We're about to get hair and makeup done. Would you mind getting us some tea?"

"No problem!" we all told her.

"Do you want mint, cinnamon, lemon zing, raspberry, or wild berry?" Isabel asked.

"With or without lemon and honey?" Kacey asked.

"Hot, warm, or cold?" I asked.

"Wow, you really know your teas!" Alexa said. "I'll have lemon zing, honey please."

We took all their orders. And we left to go to the catering tent. We ran over to the tent and then ...

BAM!

"Excuse me!" I said and looked up. I ran right into another person! I looked to see if there was whipped cream involved!

Oh! I'd run right into Claire. Claire had just stopped and was standing there with her mouth wide open. BAM! BAM! Isabel ran into me and Kacey ran into Isabel. We had all crashed.

"What—" I started to say. And then ... Oh! My! Gosh!!!!

Aaron Carter was walking by! THE Aaron Carter!!!!! In real and true life!!!!

He was being followed by about a gajillion people. They were all like, "Aaron! Aaron! Over here!" But as he walked by us he gave a little wave.

AARON CARTER WAVED AT US!

"Did Aaron Carter just wave at us?" Kacey squealed. We all looked at each other. It was true!

AARON CARTER WAVED AT THE TOO CREW! AHHHH!!!!

Kacey, Isabel and I were jumping around like crazy people! We just saw Aaron Carter! Claire was still standing there with her mouth open.

"Aaron Carter," she said, all smiley and blushy. "He's #1 on my Crush List."

We all were like WOO HOO!!!!

> *Fist, fist, hand slap, hand slap,*
> *High-five, woo hoo!*
> *TOO-Crew-Palooza!*

AARON CARTER!!!!!! In Real and True life!

Kwwwwrk! "TOO Crew?" It was Alexa. *"Would you mind adding another tea for Valerie? Just whatever kind. Thanks!"*

"Sure! And guess what! We just saw Aaron Carter!" Kacey squealed into her walkie-talkie. *"He waved right at us!"*

Kwwwwrk! "Ahhhhhhhh!" we heard back some screaming.

"Even INSPIRE is excited by that!" I said.

"Can you bring us back Aaron Carter with the tea?" Alexa asked.

"We would if we could. But we think that's beyond our job description," Isabel paged her back.

We all cracked up.

We ran into the tent and got the teas. I was still shaking from my near-Aaron experience. This day was ...

CRAZY WILD! And the concert hadn't even started yet! "Thanks," INSPIRE said when we gave them the tea.

"Sit down and hang for a little bit," said Eden.

"We don't want to be in your way," Claire said. "We're here if you need help with anything."

"Oh, just hang," Morgan said. "Our hair stylist and makeup artist are on their way and we're just hanging out doing our thing."

Alexa was in one corner of the trailer, practicing a dance move. "I keep goofing up this one," she said. "Gotta keep trying ..."

"We all do different things before the show begins," Sabrina said. "Alexa works on her dance moves. Eden sings scales to get her voice ready. Morgan's usually talking to everyone. I read a book. Or take a nap!"

"I love your t-shirts," Sabrina said. "How they say TOOPALOOZA TOO CREW on the back? That's cool."

"Want to see what we're wearing at the show today?" Eden asked. "Our outfits are hanging on this door."

Cool!

"This is mine," Eden said. She held up a green tank, dark blue and green jacke, and matching sporty pants. "This one is Sabrina's." Sabrina was going to wear a white and blue shirt, and a blue flippy skirt. Morgan was going to wear an army green shirt and matching cargoes. And Alexa's outfit was a blue and green jacket, and jeans with patches on them.

Way cool!

"Aren't they so cool?! We love 'em! Limited Too gave them to us to wear," Alexa said all excited like!!

"You guys will look great," Isabel said.

"And Isabel knows," I said. "She is practically a fashion designer already!"

"We're so psyched," Alexa said. "This is the luckiest day of my life. Oh! That reminds me. I need to put on my lucky birthstone ring."

She showed us a ring with a green stone.

"My aunt gave it to me for good luck," Alexa said. "And it's working!"

Knock! Knock! Val came in.

"Time to get your hair and makeup done," she said to INSPIRE. You're going to have some photo ops. Runners, why don't you take a break for awhile. We'll call you on the walkie-talkies when we need to."

OK!

"I don't think we were very helpful," Claire worried.

"Well, we did what they asked us to do," Isabel said. "And we'll go back and help more later."

"What do you guys want to do?" Kacey asked.

"How about we start filming!" I said. "We can hit TOO-U!"

YEAH! Everyone was into that!

chapter 10

"We're heading into TOO-U, the exciting interactive area of Toopalooza. We can't wait to see what's in here. All we know is that there's a bunch of stuff for girls to do ... so let's go on in and see what we can do!!!"

"OK, guys, I'm going to keep the camera rolling!" I announced.

COOL! There were all these tents and booths everywhere!!!

"Where do you want to go first??!!" Kacey squealed.

We heard music cranking up. ♪ ♪ ♪ A ton of girls were racing around.

"Excuse me," I said. I stopped a couple girls who were with some parents. "I'm making a tape for Limited Too about the concert. Can you tell me your names and what you're excited about today?"

"I'm Lyndsie! I can't wait to see Aaron Carter!!! I looooooove Aaron Carter!"

"I'm Emma! I'm excited to see the whole show!"

"I'm Kayla! I found out they're doing makeovers here! I want a makeover!"

"Thanks, guys!" I said. And we walked on.

"Let's try that one first," Isabel said. We ran over and into the ...

FRIENDSHIP AREA

The sign said World's Largest Bracelet. We were going to make it with CLIKITS™!

"Welcome," a woman told us. "Toopalooza is the kick-off for what is going to be the world's largest bracelet. Every girl here can click together her own pieces and then attach them to the giant bracelet. Then the bracelet will travel to different places all over where other girls will attach their own sections. Until it becomes ... the World's Largest Bracelet!!!

"Cool!" I said into the videocamera. "I'm going to make my part blue."

"Wow, we are practically the first girls to be doing this," Claire said, clik-ing pink and purple. "That's really cool. I wonder how big this thing's going to get?"

"And look," I said. "We also get to take some for ourselves. Isabel, will you clip some of these in my hair? Please?!"

"Yeah!" she laughed. "After I finish making this belt chain."

"I want to make a picture frame," Claire said. "And I'll put a picture of all four of us in it."

Awwwww!

Isabel clipped an orange flower and a blue star into my hair.
Cute!

"OK if we go film some girls now?" I asked Claire.

"Hi! I'm Mackenzie. I just made my own necklace."

"And it's so cute! I'm her friend Jacki. I want her to make me one, too!"

"I'm Brianna, and I just put my pink and orange piece on! I helped start the world's biggest bracelet!!!"

OK, we're getting our badges punched right now. Because everytime you visit a new pavilion, you get your badge punched and then CLIKITS pieces to click on your badge. And after you get all your CLIKITS pieces, then you get a prize!

chapter 11

Kwwwwrk!

"Hi, it's Alexa! We probably have about 20 more minutes getting ready. Can you make it back then?"

"Sure," Isabel said into the walkie-talkie. *"No problem."*

MUSIC AREA

"Welcome to TWISTER MOVES! I'm DJ Trey, your TWISTER MOVES DJ," a guy announced over a microphone.

"I'm Trina, your other DJ!" a girl announced. "And you girls are the next group!"

We all took a spot on a mat. The mat had different colored circles.

"Oh! I should probably film this instead," Claire said, leaving her mat and going to the side with the video camera.

"We need one more player to join this group!" DJ Trina called.

"I'm in!" a girl called out. Oh that voice sounded familiar. Ugh! Piper!

Piper came and took Claire's spot near me, Kacey, and Isabel.

"You're about to be crushed," Piper said to me. "I just auditioned to dance in a national commercial. I'm sure you'll be seeing me on TV soon."

"Oh? For Taco Tiko? Are you a dancing burrito?" Isabel asked her, all innocent.

Piper gave her a look.

But wait! We're about to start!!!

"When you hear me, step with your left foot," DJ Trey said over the microphone.

"When you hear me, step with your right foot," DJ Trina said over the microphone. Here were the other rules they said:

☆ They would be calling out colors.
★ We had to put one of our feet on the color they called out.
☆ If we goof up, they'll tell us. And we move off to the side.
☆ The last girl out there is the winner!!!

"That would be me!" Piper said confidently, flipping her hair back like she was all cool.

"Show us what you got!" DJ Trey yelled.

"Ready? Go!" DJ Trina yelled.

"Red! Purple! Green!"

I started jumping around ...

"Blue! Purple! Purple!"

OK wait ... was that left or right foot? Um ... OK ... left foot ...

"ACK!" I was yelling. And I was falling! Ka-splat! In a tangle of legs, I was DOWN!

"Girl with the ponytails, sorry! You're OUT!" DJ Trey announced.

Whoops! But no big surprise, right? Me being me and all. I went over to the side.

It was fun anyway. I was cracking up!!! I walked off to the side of the mats. But then I heard a voice calling over to me.

"Can't you do anything without falling over?" Piper asked, flipping her hair.

My face turned bright red. Not really. Thanks for reminding me.

"What did Piper say to you?" Claire asked me.

"Oh, nothing," I said. Too embarrassing!

"Well, it sure made Isabel mad," Claire said.

Oh! Isabel was looking at Piper like, Grrrrrr!

"Ready? Go?" DJ Trina announced over the microphone.

Red! Green! Blue! Green! Green!

Kacey was bouncing all over the place! Isabel was dancing! Piper was dancing! Claire was filming! I was cheering!

Go Kacey! Go Isabel!

"OK! You're out!" DJ Trey told a girl with short blond hair. Then another girl was out! Then another one!

Kacey, Isabel, and Piper were still in!

Blue! Purple! Red! Red! Another girl out! Another one!

"You're out!" DJ Trina pointed to Kacey.

OOOOOH, shoot!

Now it was down to a girl with black curly hair, Isabel, and Piper! Red! Green! Purple! Purple! Then the other girl was out!

"A little friendly competition between our finalists!" DJ Trey announced over his microphone!

Piper gave Isabel a look. A really MEAN look.

Or, a not so friendly competition. Isabel just smiled.

"Ready? Go! Blue! Purple! Green! Red!"

Faster! Faster! Their feet were flying! Piper and Isabel were jumping and dancing and Ohmigosh! What was going to happen! Who would win! Come on, Isabel! Come on!!!

"Blue! Red! Purple and ..."

Piper was looking at Isabel! Her feet were getting faster! Her looks were getting meaner! She flipped her hair back and whoops, her hair flipped into her eyes!

Flip! Whack! Ow!!! She grabbed her eye! And ...

Piper stumbled! She missed the purple!!!!

And Isabel danced on!!!

"OHHHH!!! Girl with the blonde hair! You are OUT! The winner is, the girl with the "I" on her shirt!!!!"

ISABEL WON!!! ISABEL WON!!!! SHE BEAT PIPER!!!

I ran over to Isabel! We were all jumping around! Yay! Yayyyy!

Piper stomped away. Sorry, Piper! Buh-bye.

"Great job to everyone! You're all winners! Everyone wins a prize!" DJ Trey said.

"That was awesome!" Kacey said.

"I was a nervous wreck," Claire said, all excited like. "I think the video is going to be all shaky! But I caught it all on film!"

"Isabel, you so rock," I told her while we got our prizes.

"Thanks," she said. She was smiling. "That was fun. But let's move on!" Isabel pointed in another corner. There was a big see-through container with lots of stuff in it ...

"Whoa, check this out!" Kacey said. "Massive HITCLIP-o-rama!"

"There are more than 38,000 HITCLIPS chips in there, girls," the woman told us. "Feel free to take some ..."

Claire reached in and took one out.

"Oh, take a handful," said the woman. "They're free."

Woo hoo! We all reached in and grabbed some. Awesome! I would have the best HITCLIP collection. And then I thought of my friends from home. Nah, I'd share these. I got one for Danielle, Haley, Jordan, Petie, and Sara. And, if she's nice when I get back, I'll even give one to Brittany.

"OK, Claire, get the camera! I need to interview some girls," I said.

"Hi, I'm Caitlyn and I just beat my friend in the TWISTER MOVES game, ha ha!"

"This is Adrienne and next time I'm gonna win! We're going to go play again!"

DANCE AREA

"I vote we go there, next," Isabel said. The music was cranking in the Reebok area. We walked in and saw a woman standing on a little stage. She was about to teach the audience some dance moves in a huge area. The music was cranking.

I remembered what Piper said: "Can't you do anything without falling over?"

I think I'll just sit this one out. I moved off to the side.

Through the viewer I saw Kacey, Isabel, and Claire following the instructor's steps. They were dancing! They were movin!

They were groovin! Kacey and Claire were smiling. Isabel was turning around and giving me a look like ... Maddy! Get out here, too!

I shook my head, No. But they were like Come ON, Maddy!

Ohhhhhhkay. I went out there, too. But I was stressed out! All these steps! All these moves! Left foot! Right foot. No, left! No right! Ack! I was feeling stupid but then ...

Left foot ... right foot. Left, left ... hands up ... Hey I GOT IT!!

I WAS DOING IT! I WAS WORKING IT! OH YEAH!

And then ... BAM! Somebody bumped into me!

Wait! That's right! SHE bumped into me!"

"Sorry!" the girl said. "I was on the wrong foot!"

I WASN'T THE ONE STEPPING ON ANYONE'S FOOT! FOR A CHANGE!

"No problem at all!" I told her, smiling and dancing away. The music stopped! Wooooo hooo! Kacey and Isabel faced me and we all were like, YEAH!

"That was the first time I wish I had a video camera on when

I was dancing," I said. "Hey, where's Claire?"

"Guess what," Claire smiled, holding up the camera. "I filmed that."

"Just remember that smile when you try out for cheerleading Maddy!" Isabel said. "That rocked!"

FASHION AREA

"Let's go to the Limited Too area!" Kacey said.

"Let's play the game first!" Kacey said. There were all these mannequins around. They were dressed in different outfits. Each one had a tag on it with a question.

"Hi girls," the Too worker said to us. "Go to each mannequin and answer the question. Once we get all the answers we get a prize! Let's see who can finish first!"

OK! Ready ... go! Isabel and I ran over to one mannequin! Kacey and Claire over to another! We were running all over like crazy! I was writing my answers like crazy!

Only one more left! I ran over to my last mannequin and ...

"Last one!" Kacey yelled.

"I'm going to get it!" I yelled back, laughing.

I was going to win! I was going to ...

BAM!

Run into the mannequin ... WHOA!!!!!!! Oh no! The mannequin was falling over! I was grabbing onto her!

"Hang on, Maddy! Hang on!" Isabel was yelling. The mannequin tipped left! And then right! And then ....

I got her balanced! She didn't fall over!!! WHEW!!!!

"Ohmigosh," Kacey said. "I thought for sure that mannequin was going to crash hard!"

"Nice save, Maddy!" Isabel said.

"Whew!" I said. "I don't know how I did that!"

"Want to find out?" Claire said. "I caught it all on videotape."

"Oh noooooo," I groaned. "You filmed that?"

"Well, Lauren said they wanted footage of what really happens," Claire said. "Oh OK, it was pretty funny. Look."

I peeked into the camera. Ack! I said. But I was laughing.

Claire, Kacey, and Isabel started watching the video and laughing, too. But wait! Aha! Now was my chance. I ran back to the mannequin. I answered the question. And...

"While you guys were laughing at me ... I won!!!" I yelled. "Woo hoo!" I did a victory dance.

But—not too close to the mannequin.

Everyone finished their game and we went to collect our prize. A CD!

"Try out our glamour stations," a Too worker said to us. She pointed to tables set up with stuff like body glitter and lip gloss.

"I was going to come over and offer to do your hair in a fun style," said one of the Too workers. "But it looks like someone good already got to you!"

"Yeah," I told her, pointing at Isabel. "She's awesome at doing hair."

I put on some blueberry swirly lip gloss. And sprayed myself with a powdery scent.

"Tada!" I said, looking at myself in the mirror.

"OK, NOW I want to be videotaped!" I said. "Looking like this!"

We all struck a pose! And then ...

Fist, fist, hand slap, hand slap,
High-five, woo hoo!
TOO-Crew-Palooza!

"If you're ready, go on over and learn what it's like to be a model," the woman working there told us. "And get some tips."

"OK, could I have done that before I was at the catazine shoot?" I laughed, while we waited in line. "Maybe then I would have known what I was doing!"

We were up! All four of us went in together.

They showed a group of us how to walk like a model. How to pose. How to look at the audience. And how to work it! A couple other girls went first. I filmed them walking down the catwalk like they were models.

"Hi, I'm Jasmine. That felt like I was a real model!"

"I'm going to go get my picture taken like this! Check out my new hairstyle! I'm Andrea!"

"OK, girls. You're up there next."

The music started! And we started walking down the catwalk. I was up first.

"Modeling the latest styles in TOO Crew Wear by Claire, it's Maddy Elizabeth Sparks!" I announced.

"Woo hoo!" Kacey, Isabel and Claire clapped and cheered for me. I posed. I blew kisses.

"Go, Maddy!" Kacey cheered. "Work it, girl!"

I catwalked down the catwalk. I gave them my best smile. I did my best supermodel pose.

"This is the part where I usually trip," I announced. "So I'm getting off, now!" I hopped down.

Claire held up the videocamera.

"Ack!" I said. "Tell me you didn't tape that!"

Claire just smiled.

"Oh noooo!" But I was laughing. What the heck.

"Now, we want to take a picture of you supermodels!" one of

the women working said.

"Here's where we'll get a picture for your frame!" Kacey said to Claire.

We jumped in together. Claire put her arm around me and Kacey. Kacey put her arm around Isabel. We all squinched together ....

"Get ready, girls! And say ..."

"Too-Crew-PALOOZA!" we all yelled. We were laughing! We were smiling! And ...

"Wait!" Claire said. "Maddy, you have to push us all over. Just for old times sake."

"Are you serious!" I said, laughing. OK! Here I go! I leaned into Claire. Who leaned into Kacey. Who fell over onto Isabel. And who took us all down with her!

 CLICK!

The moment was captured forever.

chapter 12

Kwwwwrk! "Hi TOO Crew! It's Alexa! We're ready for some help, OK?"

"Be right there!" Isabel said into her walkie-talkie. Claire put the videocamera back into the case. We all went to INSPIRE's trailer and knocked. We went in. Everyone looked great!!!!

"We are made up and hair-ed up," said Eden. "Looks like you guys are a little, too!"

"First we're going to sign autographs," Alexa said. "Then we go to the Media Tent. That's where we have to do interviews."

"You guys are going to come to the autograph thing and watch us. You can tape it if you want," Morgan told Claire.

"Thanks!" Claire said, taking out the videocamera.

"Wait! I can't forget my lucky ring," Alexa said.

"I have a lucky choker," I told her. We are so alike!

We all headed over to the autographing table. Val came with us.

"Are you nervous? About being interviewed and autographs and stuff?" I asked Alexa.

"Yeah," said Alexa. "I get kinda nervous. I worry about what they're going to ask me. Sabrina gets nervous. Eden and Morgan are like yay! Not nervous! They like that stuff!"

I always worried about sounding stupid, too. I was a lot like Alexa.

Lauren met us at the autographing table.

"INSPIRE, you'll sit at the table doing your thing," Lauren said. "TOO Crew, each of you stand next to one of the INSPIRE girls. You're in charge of handing her a CD to be autographed every time a new girl comes up."

I went over and stood by Alexa. Kacey stood next to Eden, Isabel next to Morgan. Claire was next to Sabrina. And then ...

Here come the fans!!!!

All these girls came up! They got in a line! Some with their friends! Some with their moms! Girls everywhere! Getting autographs from INSPIRE!

Everytime Alexa autographed a CD, I gave her a new one. She signed so many autographs I thought her hand would fall off.

"Wow," I said to her. "That's a lot of people. And you're still smiling and signing!"

"Every fan is special," Alexa told me. "I mean, without the fans we wouldn't be here, right?"

They signed and signed and signed and signed for their fans!!!! And I interviewed some more girls for Tape-a-palooza.

"Hi! I'm Kennedy! INSPIRE just signed a CD for me! I love their new CD! I'm so excited!!!"

"I'm Ilana. I don't know too much about INSPIRE yet, 'cuz they're new. But they were sooo nice. I can't wait to listen to their music."

"OK, we are finished!" Val said. "It's time to get ready for the show! INSPIRE, back to the trailer to get ready."

Alexa, Eden, Morgan, and Sabrina came over and we all said goodbye.

"Good luck!" I told them. "I can't wait to see the show!"

IT'S TRUE! IT'S ALMOST TIME FOR THE CONCERT!!!

"This day has been unbelievable," I said to Kacey as we were packing up CD's. "And we haven't even seen the concert yet."

"Major blast," Kacey agreed. "But I think Claire is ready to see the concert. Hey, Claire! What's the countdown to Aaron Carter?"

"Forty two minutes and 12 seconds until the show starts!" Claire said. "Oh my gosh! Forty two minutes and 11 seconds now! I'm going to faint!"

Hee! Claire is so crushing on Aaron Carter!

"Oh no!" I said, bending down. "It's Alexa's lucky ring. She must have dropped it!"

"We better bring it back to her trailer," Kacey said. "We don't want her to think she lost it forever!"

Isabel got on the walkie-talkie and told Alexa we had her ring. We headed over to the trailers. Val met us outside.

"Thank you, girls," she said. "Alexa had just noticed it was missing! Whew!"

"Glad to help," I said.

Yay! We really helped today! First, Nina Miles (ugh). Then helping INSPIRE. The videotape. And now even rescuing Alexa's ring!

"And now, we get to relax," said Kacey. "And hang out and enjoy the show!"

And then we heard a huge noise.

BANG! CRASH!

chapter 13

"What was that?" Claire asked.

CRASH! BANG!

"I think it's coming from Nina Miles' trailer," Isabel said.

We looked over. And there was Felicia, Nina's manager. She was banging on the trailer door!

"Nina! Let me in! Right this second!" she was yelling.

"Oopsie," Kacey said. "Let's just keep on walking. Not our business."

We started walking by realllll fast. La la la. Didn't hear a thing.

"Girls! TOO Crew!" Felicia said, all flipping out. "There's a big problem. Can you get your person from Limited Too to help?"

"What's the matter?" Claire asked.

"Nina is throwing things!" Felicia said.

SMASH!

"And breaking them," Kacey whispered.

"Why?" Claire asked Felicia.

"Because Ursula didn't show up!"

"Who's Ursula?" I whispered to Isabel. She shrugged.

Then we heard Nina yelling from inside the trailer. "I'm not doing the show! Not without Ursula here!"

"Ursula is Nina's hair stylist," Felicia said. "Without her, Nina can't get her hair done."

"Can't you just get another stylist for now?" Kacey asked. "I mean, just for today?"

"I've checked with all the other stylists here," Felicia said. "They're busy with their own clients."

"They probably said no way when they heard it was for Nina Miles," Kacey whispered to me.

Yeah, really! She was such a ... diva!

"I won't go on! Cancel my act!" Nina yelled. "I'm not going on without Ursula doing my hair! That's final! Tell the concert people I'm not going on!"

"Nina," said Felicia. "You have a commitment to this concert."

"I don't care!" Nina said. "You can't make me!"

I looked at Kacey, Isabel, and Claire.

"We'll call Lauren," Claire said. She started to talk into the walkie-talkie.

"Nina, it's great exposure!" Felicia was begging. "This concert is great for your career!"

Nina was all No! No way! Nope! Nope! Nope!

"Lauren's not answering," Claire reported.

"What about all the girls who want to see Nina?" I asked. "Doesn't she care about her fans?"

"Guess not," Kacey said. "Maybe we should just leave and let her ruin her own career."

But Kacey didn't leave. We all stood there.

"We've got to help," said Isabel. "It's for the good of the show."

"But how?" Claire asked.

Really! But how?!?!?!?! And then ...

I looked at Kacey's twists. At Claire's French braids. I GOT IT!

"Isabel can do Nina's hair." I said.

"What?" Kacey said. "You think Nina will let her?"

"Hey, Isabel is great with hair. We can try," I said. I knocked on the trailer door.

"Go away!" Nina's voice screamed. "I'm not doing the show and that's final!"

Hm.

"It's One, Two, Three, and Four," I yelled out. "We have an idea."

"I don't need any more tea! Go away."

"Nina," Claire said. "We have an idea. It can't hurt to let us in!"

The door slowly opened. Nina let us in and then turned away. It looked like she'd been crying. She ran to the back of the trailer.

Oh, man! And Piper was still there, sitting on the sofa. Although, she wasn't looking like she was having much fun. She was looking all freaked out.

"Nina's flipped," Piper whispered to us. "And she won't let me leave! I'm trapped in this trailer with a crazy musician!"

"Nina, we have a plan," Kacey said nicely. "Number Three can help you. She can do your hair."

"What?" Nina said. "I'm not letting you runners near my hair."

"She's really good–" Claire said. But Nina interrupted her.

"Forget it!" Nina said. "I'm not doing the show. No way. Just forget it. And hey! Piper! Where do you think you're going?"

We looked at Piper. She was trying to sneak out the door.

"Um, I gotta go?" she said.

"No! Stay." Nina said.

Ooh! She was even ordering Piper around! Piper slunk back in and sat down.

"There are all these girls out there counting on you to be onstage! They don't care if your hair is perfect," I said.

"I don't go out there unless my hair is great," Nina said. "And that's final."

"Look, Nina," I said. "Isabel is amazing at hair. Look at all of ours. She did mine in like three seconds."

Nina took a look at me. She looked around at us. She sniffed. And then she said it.

"Oh, all right. Get to work."

"Butterfly clip!" Isabel commanded.

"Check!" Kacey handed it to her.

"Round brush!" Isabel said.

"Here!" Claire gave it to her.

"Rubber bands!" "Comb!" "Hairspray!"

Major hair stylage!

Isabel was like ... Clip! Brush! Fluff! Spray!

Claire and I sat to the side, holding our breath. Felicia and Piper sat to the side, not saying a thing. And then ...

"OK," Isabel said. "Nina, turn around ..."

Nina turned toward us and ... WOW!

"Wow!" Claire and I said.

Even Piper said, "Whoa!"

Nina looked amazing! Her hair was done in braids and loops and ...

"You look like a star," I said.

"Let me look in my mirror," Nina demanded. She stomped over to the mirror. And she looked. And ....

"Oh," she said. "Huh."

And she smiled! And then she said ....

"We better get backstage, right, Felicia? Are you trying to make me late for the show or something?"

Felicia let out this huge sigh like, PHEW!!!!!!!

YAY! NINA MILES WAS GOING ON!

"Nina, wait! Do you think you could be a doll and ask Number Three to do my hair, too?" a voice asked.

PIPER!!!!

Piper wanted Isabel to do her hair, too!

Oh nooooo! But then ...

Kwwwwrk! **"TOO Crew!"** It was Lauren on the walkie-talkie. **"The show's going to start soon. Meet me near the stage!"**

"Well, have to go!" Kacey said. "Buh-bye!"

We ran out of there as fast as we could!!!!

"Isabel, you so rock!" I told her as we were running.

"You totally saved the day!" Kacey said.

"Thanks," Isabel said, smiling.

And Lauren was waiting for us! We ran up to her. "Anyone want to see a concert?" she asked.

ME!!! And Kacey! And Isabel! And Claire!

We all went ... YEAH!!!!!

> *Fist, fist, hand slap, hand slap,*
> *High-five, woo hoo!*
> *TOO-Crew-Palooza!*

chapter 14

"I'm Kayleigh! And I can not wait to see Aaron Carter!"

"I'm Leah. I totally love Ashlee Simpson and she's going to be right on that stage! I'm so happy!"

"I'm going to see Nick Cannon! I am going to FREAK out! AHH-HHH! Oh! My name's Saipriya."

Claire and I were videotaping all these girls. They were sitting! They were standing! They were jumping up and down! All over the lawn in front of the stage.

"I've never been to a concert before! I'm I am soooo excited! I mean, Mandy Moore??! Yay!"

"See my Jhene t-shirt? I'm her biggest fan! I'm Victoria!"

OK. It was totally crazy! Totally exciting! Thousands of girls. Who were so excited to see everyone in this show!

"I'm Justine. And hel-lo? Jessica Simpson? LOVE her!"

"I'm Nikki! Just like Nikki Cleary! Yay!"

"My name's Mollie! And I love Nina Miles!"

I looked over at Isabel after that one! If she hadn't done Nina's hair, this girl would have been seriously bummed!

And any minute now ... the show was going to start.

Kwrrk! "TOO Crew! Please head toward the left of the stage in the blue area."

OK! Lauren was calling us on the walkie-talkie. Kacey, Isabel, Claire and I made our way through the girls. We went to the blue area. And there was Lauren! We followed her to the very front row.

"This is the area where the contest winners and their guests get to sit," Lauren said. She pointed to some girls who were all dancing around. They had backpacks and I recognized goodie bags on the ground next to them. Contest winners! How cool is that! The stage was like right in front of their faces. They'd get to see everything wayyyyy close!

"And I saved a little room for the TOO Crew," Lauren told us. "Make yourselves comfortable and enjoy the show."

Lauren walked away.

And Kacey, Isabel, and I looked at each other. OK, we were in the front row? Oh. My. GOSH!!!!!!!!!!

AHHHHHHHHHHHHHHHHHH!

Kacey stuck out her fist. Then Isabel, then Claire. And then me!

Fist, fist, hand slap, hand slap,
High-five, woo hoo!
TOO-Crew-Palooza!

!!!!!!!!!!!!!!!!!!!

It was time for me to do some *Tape-a-Palooza!*

"Filming live from Too-Palooza, in the front row ... Let's turn around and take a look at the crowd ... Girls everywhere! Dancing! Screaming! Jumping up and down! Any minute now, the concert is about to start ...."

And all of a sudden the crowd went WAY CRAZY!!!!! Because AARON CARTER was on stage!

I looked over at Claire. She was soooo happy. I was so happy! We were all so happy!

The hosts were introduced. Aaron! Then Ashlee Simpson from 7th *Heaven*, Ohmigosh!! Then, the winner of the contest got to co-host with them! She was up there, too!

Wow! Wow and Wow!!!

My first concert! And it was ...

MAJOR!!!!!!!

And then they announced the opening act ... PLAY!!!!

The four singers in Play ran up on stage! Like, right in front of my face! And they started singing ...

Claire was shooting video of everything around us. I could see girls dancing and going way crazy. They were screaming PLAY! PLAY!

AND SO WAS I!!! Dancing! Singing along! It was AWESOME!

And when Play was over, they announced that the next group up was pretty new. Making their national debut, it was the *TOO's U-Pick Challenge* winners, the group ...

INSPIRE!

They ran out and waved to the crowd. And so on the same stage as Aaron, Ashlee, and Play ... there were Eden, Morgan, Sabrina and Alexa!!!

"It's awesome to be here at Toopalooza!" Eden yelled into her microphone.

"And you know what? We wouldn't be here if it wasn't for girls just like YOU!" Morgan said.

"Because you voted us the winners of the *TOO's U-Pick*

Challenge Contest!" Sabrina said.

"And we want to shout out to a couple girls who especially helped us get here," Alexa said. "So come on up here on stage, TOO Crew ... Kacey ... Isabel ... Claire ... and Maddy!!!!"

OK ...

HUH?!?!?!

Did she just say what I thought she said? The TOO Crew? Maddy meaning ME, Maddy?

I looked at Claire. Claire looked at Kacey. Kacey looked at Isabel. And Isabel nodded and went, "Let's go!"

The security people helped us up the stairs on to the stage. I was shaking! I was like Ohmigosh! I was like ...

WOW! This is what it looks like from the stage! I peeked behind stage. Oh! I saw Aaron Carter back there. OK, I am going to FAINT!!!

I looked out over the crowd. There were girls everywhere! Thousands of them! We all waved. And they waved back at us!!!

"Turn on the camera, Claire! Get this on film!" I whispered.

I looked at all those girls smiling! And I noticed one of them who wasn't ... it was Piper! Piper was way back in the crowd! I wonder if she was thinking, Hey! How'd that girl who trips over everything get up there? How come I'm not up there! I am the Taco Tiko Princess, you know!

"See these girls up here?" Alexa said. "These girls are girls just like you. And we are so grateful to them. And they helped us get the honor of being the *TOO's U-Pick Challenge* Contest winners! So thanks, TOO Crew!"

"I can't believe this is happening!" I said out loud. Not that anyone could hear me! 'Cuz everyone started chanting:

INSPIRE! INSPIRE! INSPIRE!

The security guys had us sit at the edge of the stage. And INSPIRE began to sing.

Think you're facing ... the world all alone?
It's all going by without you ...
Think that things will never be good again?

I thought about that day when I was really bummed out. I turned on the radio and heard this song. I didn't even know who the group was! But the song totally cheered me up. And now, I was sitting on a stage with the real and totally live group. In front of thousands of girls. At Toopalooza.

You just never know what could happen to you!!!!

Kacey put her arm around me. I put my other arm around Isabel. She put her arm around Claire. We started swaying back and forth. The TOO Crew, totally on stage at Toopalooza.

You think you're alone, girl? Just listen to this song, girl!
And see that's all so wrong, girl ... 'cuz ...

And we all started singing along.

Things are looking up! Oh yeah!
Things are LOOKING UP! Yeah ...

Things couldn't be looking any better!

chapter 15

The TOO Crew and Lauren were all sitting around the hotel room VCR. She turned the video on so we could watch the videotape. Here goes ...!

OK, there was my thumb. Covering up the camera. Oopsie.

"Whoops! I thought I deleted that!" I said.

Phew! Thumb was gone. Claire had taken control. We all watched as we were getting Toopalooza on tape! We were walking through LEGOLAND California for the first time!

I remembered how exciting it was getting there! Sooo cool!

Then we were running around TOO-U!

Oops!

There was me falling in TWISTER MOVES.

"Let's delete that, too," I suggested.

"Naaah, it's hilarious!" said Isabel.

"Is that Piper?" Lauren asked, peering closely at the girls

dancing around on tape.

And then there's the Isabel vs. Piper Danceoff!!!! Woo hoo!
Isabel winning!

Oops! There was me, almost knocking the mannequin over at
the Fashion Pavillion. And then there I was interviewing
some girls ... and I had whipped cream on my forehead!

Wait? I interviewed girls with whipped cream on my forehead?
Ack!!!

"AUGH!" I said. "I can't watch this! Too painful! This is like
Maddy's Most Embarrassing Bloopers Video! The Toopalooza
edition!!!"

"Oh, Maddy," Claire said. "That's so not true."

"Well, maybe a little true," Isabel agreed with me. "But look at
all the times you didn't klutz out. Like, you did learn those
dance moves in the dance pavilion really great."

"You walked down the catwalk without tripping!" Kacey said.

"You sat on the edge of the stage without falling off," Claire
said, seriously.

"Ohmigosh!" I said "I never even thought of that! I would

have been freaking out if I'd thought of that!"

"See?" Isabel said. "Just focus on the good parts."

"Maddy," Lauren said. "I didn't pick you to host the video because you're perfect. We like the real Maddy. Sure, you fall over. Sure you goof up. But that's what happens to everyone sometimes."

"Yeah," Isabel said. "Sometimes you screw up. Sometimes you rock."

"It never happens to you, Isabel," I said. Isabel was always so cool! So calm! So in control!

"That's so not true!" Kacey said. "You haven't heard the stories her Gran was telling us on the plane. Isabel has had her embarrassing moments! I'll tell you later."

"Yikes!" Isabel laughed. "I was hoping everyone forgot those."

"So see, Maddy? It's all in the attitude afterwards?" Lauren said. "And you guys should be proud of yourselves for having a great attitude today."

So ... half the video is me being embarrassing. And the other half is me, well, being kinda ... I don't know ... cool, I guess. That pretty much sums me up I guess. That is really me!

Hey!

This Is Really Me. That's what my speech in school is supposed to be about. Actually, it wasn't a bad thing I didn't get to give it the other day. It wasn't very good. I had to give it when I got back. But I could write another one.

I thought about how totally embarrassed I was when I left Language Arts class. 'Cuz I tripped and fell like a SuperKlutz.

But sometimes I am a SuperKlutz! And sometimes ... I'm not! That Is Really ME!!!

My speech! I could do my speech for Language Arts on how I really am. A mix of all these things. I could even bring the videotape to show my class. I mean, they already saw the SuperKlutz Maddy totally humiliate myself! I could be like, Yup, that's part of the Real Me!

And then they'd stop laughing at me. They'd be laughing with me. And all that kind of thing, blah blah. But seriously, in my speech I could be like, Hey! Yeah that was embarrassing when I flew across the room! Whoops! But I can always recover! Right?

That could be a good speech. Yup.

I turned back to the videotape.

It was showing the concert!!!! There was Aaron Carter! So

totally cute!

(Claire went like this when she saw him, Ahhhhhhhhhhhh!)

There's Ashlee Simpson! There's Nina Miles heading backstage.

"Nina's hair looks great," Lauren told Isabel. "Maddy told me how you did Nina's hair and saved the day."

There's Play!!!!! There's INSPIRE! And there we are!!!!

We watched through Claire's eyes on the tape from when we were on stage with INSPIRE. You could see kajillions of girls singing and dancing and screaming and waving and smiling! That was so cool.

And then Mandy Moore, Wow!!! She's like a singer and a major movie STAR!

Then my interviews in the crowd.

"OK, tell me what you liked best about this concert?" I was asking some girl.

"AHHHHHHHHHHHHH!"

"Um, can you tell us anything else?" I asked her.

"AHHHHHHHHH!!!!!"

We were all cracking up watching that!

"That girl was seriously excited!" I said. "All she said was ... 'AHHHHH!' OK, here come some other girls I talked to."

"I can't believe I can see real live celebrities! There in front of me!"

"I practically lost my voice already from screaming so loud!"

"There's so much noise! It's cra-zay!"

"This is way incredibly COOL!"

KNOCK! KNOCK KNOCK!

Someone was knocking at the door!

"Girls," Lauren said, getting up and turning off the TV. "We'll watch the rest later. This is a great job of capturing the show. It's a great mix of seeing Toopalooza through your own eyes, as well as through other girls eyes."

Oh! Yay!

"And now, I have a little surprise for you girls." She opened the door. And in walked ... INSPIRE!

"Hiiiiiiiiii!" said Eden! And Morgan! And Sabrina! And Alexa!

"Thank you sooooo much for having us on stage," I said. "That was so unbelievably unbelievable!"

"You guys were so awesome!" Kacey said.

"That was a total blast," Eden said. "We're still pumped up!"

"We're taking off," Morgan said. "But first, we wanted to stop by and say good-bye."

"And," Sabrina said. "We all have something we want to give you."

Alexa pulled out some little boxes.

"Lauren thought it would be cool if we gave this to you," Alexa said. "To remember this day!"

She handed them out. We opened them up and took out our new charms.

"A little music CD!" I said. I looked closely, putting it on.

"For your first concert with Limited Too," Lauren said. "You should be proud of yourselves. You had some challenging work ..."

I looked at Kacey. I knew what she was thinking. Nina Miles!

"And you worked hard and kept a positive attitude," Lauren

finished.

"Check this out," Morgan said. She showed us a silver chain attached to her belt loops. She had a CD charm on it, too! And so did Eden! And Sabrina! And Alexa!

"Lauren gave us a charm, too! We'll never forget this day!" Alexa said.

Awwwww!!!!!

"Hey, we should teach you something else to remember Toopalooza by," I said. I held out my fist. The TOO Crew came over and we showed them the moves.

"OK, got it!" said Eden.

"Yeah, yeah," grumbled Alexa, but kind of jokey. "You always get it. Give me a chance to practice here!" She tried the moves a couple times.

"OK," she said. "Got it!"

"Wait, can I videotape us?" I asked everyone.

SURE!

Lauren picked up the video camera and started to film us.

Eden! Morgan! Sabrina! And Alexa!

Kacey! Isabel! Claire! And ME!!!!

> *Fist, fist, hand slap, hand slap,*
> *High-five, woo hoo!*
> *TOO-Crew-Palooza!*

Happy Face Rating:

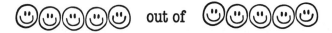 out of

The end ...

OK! But not really! 'Cuz more good stuff's going to happen!

Stay TUNED!

the **too crew's**
stuff for you to do

Make Your Own Moves!

Isabel made up the Move for Too-Crew-Palooza. This is how it goes:

Fist, fist (we knock our fists together)
Hand slap, hand slap (we do "Slap me five!" two times)
High-five (we all high five once)
Woo hoo! (and then we yelled woo hoo!)

You can make your own to do with your friends. Mix and match some of these. Or make up your own!

High five
Low five
Slap me five
Knock fists
Jump up
Bend down
Bump hips

Fill in the Blanks ...
Toopalooza Style

We were at a concert! The crowd of _____ (plural noun) were so psyched! "Look!" _____ (friend's name) yelled, pointing to the stage. "It's _____ (celebrity!)" The music was _____ (verb-ing). We started singing our fave song about _____ (plural nouns).

We were dancing and _____ (verb-ing) around. And all of a sudden, _____ (male musician) came onstage. He said "I'm so _____(adjective) to be here. And now I want to invite someone onstage to be part of my band."

He called me up onstage! YEAH! He gave me a _____ (noun) to play. I jammed with the band. The crowd was chanting "_____!" (exclamation). And then _____ (female celebrity) came onstage. She announced I won a prize. It was a _____ (color) _____ (noun)!

"I always wanted that!" I screamed. "This is the most awesome and _____ (adjective) time I ever had!!!"

This Journal Belongs to:

Maddy Elizabeth Sparks

Hi!! Or OK, BYE! 'Cuz I gotta go. But don't worry!
Kacey and Isabel and Claire and I will be back ...
because remember what I have to do next?

I have to get ready for cheerleading tryouts! EEK!!!!
The TOO Crew is going to help me get ready to do it!

And some awesome ... amazing ... totally cool things are
going to be happening!!!

In Tuned In Episode #5! Coming exclusively to
Limited TOO!!!! Check out limitedtoo.com and get
Tuned In!

Luv ya', Maddy!